The Wooden Gun

BILL MORRISON

A Black Horse Western

ROBERT HALE · LONDON

Photoset in North Wales by
Derek Doyle & Associates, Mold, Clwyd.
Printed and bound in Great Britain by
WBC Ltd, Bridgend, Mid-Glamorgan.

ONE

'Jem! You got them stores to lift now. You hear me?'

Chris Elliot turned from shouting out through the doorway and looked sharply at the storekeeper whose smile faded as he sensed the rising irritation of his customer.

'It's OK, Mr Elliot, I can give you a hand with them ...'

His voice trailed off and he said no more as Elliot strode to the door and stood there, framed almost as a black shadow against the morning sun.

For a moment, Elliot did not move except to tilt his stetson forward slightly to shield his eyes from the glare. He took in the view of the street in a glance; the wooden sidewalks, the low wooden buildings, the townspeople sauntering by or conversing in groups; the horses hitched in the shade, the heat and the dust.

Just in front of the store, his ramshackle old buggy, long since stripped of any finery it may once have possessed, stood motionless. On the buckboard behind the aged mule, Jem still sat, waving his wooden rifle at the sky, as if to shoot down the crows which flew overhead. The imitation gun was about three feet long, covered now with scratches, notches and crudely carved shapes, mostly unrecognizable as representations of anything in particular, which Jem had cut out in those moments when his mind descended into that dreamlike state beyond the reach even of his brother.

Forcing himself not to sound angry, Elliot repeated his request for help and, as he spoke, his eyes swept past

Jem's stocky figure to the saloon some way down on the other side of the main street. There were two men standing there, one very still and upright, the other lolling forward, his elbows on the railing, grinning under his slight, dark moustache, his entire attitude one of unconcealed amusement.

'OK, Chris, I'm comin'.' Jem turned around and began to clamber down from the buggy. He was twenty-two years old, dark haired and freckled and almost handsome, but his lopsided smile, the vague look in his eyes and something about the set of his features illustrated beyond doubt the backward nature of his mind.

As Jem shuffled past him to begin the loading of the month's stores, Elliot continued in his observation of the strangers. The one who was standing stock still in the shade of the overhanging roof was obviously a half-breed, too dark for ordinary sunburn, wearing a buckskin jacket and a black hat, broad brimmed and with a feather stuck in its band. His hair was longer than that of the average white and Elliot could almost make out the shape of a necklace of some sort at his throat.

The other man wore dark clothing and carried a gun at his hip. His insolent grin had gone now and he returned Elliot's stare almost as a challenge.

The irritation that Elliot had felt at Jem's childish neglect of his task was giving way to the anger that always came to him when he believed that his younger brother was being held in contempt. Not that it happened very often. Most of the people in town and in the surrounding country knew and liked Jem and spoke to him in a kindly manner. The few who were not so kindly disposed knew better than to make any less than polite remark or gesture so long as Jem's elder brother, the ex-cavalry sergeant, who had returned from the war a sight tougher, more brittle and embittered than when he had rode off to it, was in the vicinity …

Elliot's hand fumbled in the pocket of his faded blue

army tunic, half of his mind on the cost of the stores he was about to pay for while the other half wrestled with the impulse to cross the street towards the saloon. One of the few remaining brass buttons came away in his fingers and he contemplated its dull surface for a few seconds as his thoughts went back to the tiny homestead with its parcel of worn-out soil which was the only legacy left to him when he came back to Red Creek, with his brain still full of the turmoil and savagery of the long, drawn out conflict, to find his parents now dead and his younger brother – that 'poor, soft-headed boy', as his mother had called him – living on the charity of their neighbours.

He readjusted his hat on his fair hair and shrugged off the feeling of despair that sometimes threatened to overwhelm him. He had come out of the war alive and in one piece. There were plenty of men who had not done that much. So long as Jem was around there was nothing else for it except to get what living they could from the little farm that his parents had spent so many years of hard work and hope trying to turn into something worthwhile.

He did not spare the strangers on the other side of the street another glance but went back into the store where Jem was lifting out the last sack of flour.

'That'll be twelve dollars and fifteen cents, Mr Elliot,' said the storekeeper.

It was more than Elliot had reckoned but he kept his face expressionless as he paid out the money, turning out his pockets for the last few coins. As he did so, he heard Jem's voice raised outside. Guessing what was happening, he turned and walked purposefully to the door. The dark-moustached stranger was there, one foot on the steps leading up to the sidewalk, one hand on his hip. He was leering at Jem, having decided that Elliot – who seemed to have backed off into the store – was no threat.

'Hey, that sure is a mighty fine rifle you got thar, son;

bet you kin do plenty huntin' and fightin' with that!'

'Well, no, it cain't really do no huntin' or anythin',' replied Jem, the sarcasm going over his head.

'Is that so?' queried the stranger in mock amazement. 'I coulda sworn thet was one o' them newfangled Winchester repeater rifles thet kin shoot down about a hunner an' fifty Injuns, bandits and jack-rabbits in three seconds flat ...'

'Well, no, it ain't one o' them,' stumbled Jem. 'My pa made this for me way long time ago. It don't really shoot none but sometimes I go into the woods an' blast away at rabbits an' suchlike.'

The stranger laughed, showing bad, tobacco-stained teeth.

'You're one helluva smart feller. Y'know thet? Bet you came out right top of the school in this one-horse town! Bet you ...'

The remark was never finished as Elliot's fist cracked into the stranger's mouth, sending him sprawling down the steps and into the dirt of the street. He rolled over on his hands and knees, spitting out blood. For a moment he seemed dazed, hardly able to believe what had happened, then his face became consumed with rage and he began to rise, his hand going for his gun ...

'Leave that gun be, polecat, or I'll blast you to hell!'

Elliot, having anticipated the stranger's reaction, had stepped quickly over the sidewalk, tugged out his cavalry rifle from its hiding place in the buggy and now held the man's forehead firmly in the sights.

For a second the hand still hovered as if to clutch at the butt of the revolver in spite of the danger, then the stranger thought better of it. He withdrew his hand, eyes still blazing.

'Unsling that gunbelt, you dirty-mouthed snake, slow and easy.'

The gunbelt slid to the ground. Elliot was about to order the man to step back when another voice intervened.

'It's OK, mister, this man won't give you no more trouble. Get back to that saloon, Wilson, and leave your gun where it is. I'll bring it to you – if I kin get this gentleman to part with it.'

Wilson hesitated, then walked back over the street morosely but without argument. Elliot looked at the man who had interrupted. He was mounted on a chestnut mare in quite good condition with saddle and bridle that looked almost new. What struck Elliot at once was that the man's appearance seemed at variance with his mount, his clothes being well worn and travel stained, although their general cut and style suggested that they had originally been intended for a man better off than most. His face was half concealed by a black beard, streaked with grey. His words, although seeming to attempt to pacify, lacked sincerity.

'Sorry about my man, mister, but he forgits his manners. Ain't had the advantage of good breeding. All right if he gits his gun back now? He won't reach for it again, I promise you, Mr ... sorry, we ain't been introduced. My name's Proctor – Sam Proctor – and yours ...?'

'Just keep your men well away from me – and my brother,' replied Elliot curtly.

He mounted the buggy and stirred the sleepy mule into movement. He stared straight ahead as they trundled slowly along the street, his anger still with him and aware of the curious glances of the townsfolk. As they went, Jem swung around on the buckboard, his eyes popping, his mind unable to comprehend the meaning of events. He saw the bearded man on the horse looking after them with a thoughtful expression, the half-breed still motionless in the shade, the dark, moustached man sitting on the edge of the sidewalk padding at his mouth and glaring balefully at Elliot's retreating head, the storekeeper turning back indoors, probably relieved that there had been no shooting, kids gaping, one of them putting out his tongue ....

They were silent for a time as the buggy crawled through the outskirts of the small town and turned towards home. Then Jem's dim thoughts found expression.

'Hey, what did you hit that guy for, Chris? Why d'ya hit him? He was asking about the rifle. He was sayin' about huntin'.'

'I heard what he was sayin'.' Elliot gritted his teeth, knowing the futility of trying to explain what Wilson's remarks had really meant and his own reaction to them. Jem could never understand and maybe it was just as well.

'You got to do somethin' about that temper of yours, Chris. You really got to. I remember Pa yellin' at you about that temper! He said it would git ya into trouble some day, he said, didn't he? Ya remember that don't ya?'

Elliot remembered and reflected that although Jem could often forget things that had happened only moments before, he could sometimes remember events that had long since vanished from the memories of other people.

'You got to stop takin' that dummy rifle of yours into town. I told ya before. Leave it in the house. You got work to do when we go into the town. Y'know that!'

Even as he spoke, Elliot knew that he was changing the subject in order to divert Jem from the long, confused and repetitive lecturing which he sometimes indulged in. Elliot knew it was a waste of time talking about the rifle. Jem would continue to carry it in spite of the amused and patronizing smiles that it drew from the townspeople, into which he could read nothing but friendship but which were a source of irritation to his brother. At times he had thought of getting rid of it and making some excuse to Jem for its disappearance but he could not do that. It meant too much to Jem, who had always wanted a real gun but who could never have one. It would be like giving a firearm to a six-year-old kid.

They argued for a while, Elliot with patience and Jem in his manner of childish excitement. Then they fell into a silence which lasted until noon and they were well up the little-used trail which wound its way through the valley of Red Creek between its escarpments of rock and clumps of trees, still heavy with the foliage of late summer. To the west, clouds were beginning to build up beyond the dark hills, promising the rain which had been a long time in coming and which would probably burst now at the wrong time for the bringing in of the crops which the folks of the valley had been watching turning too dry all summer.

'Hey, Chris, see what I got here!' Jem's voice broke the heavy silence as he thrust his hand under his brother's nose. Elliot pulled up sharp, the mule giving a grunt of protest.

In the palm of his hand Jem held a tiny gold nugget which glinted in the light, its surface damp with sweat.

'Where in hell did ya get that?' Elliot stared at his brother in amazement.

'Got it from an Injun. the one that came – when was it? Well, he gave it to me anyway. Only I lost it in the grass then I found it again this mornin' when you was yellin' at me to git the mule harnessed up.'

Elliot examined the nugget carefully. It wasn't worth much – just a few dollars but maybe they could sell it next time they were in town. They could get something for it at the bank very likely. He looked at Jem again, wondering with a kind of wild hope that there might be more.

'Who did you say gave you this? An Indian?'

'Yeah, I remember now. That feller called himself Half Yellow Face.' He laughed childishly at the name.

Elliot looked thoughtful. He remembered about a week ago seeing Jem leaning against the far gate talking to an Indian, a man with two feathers in his jet-black hair, who stood listening with grave attention to whatever Jem was saying to him, while his left hand held the halter of a skewbald pony. He had mounted and ridden off quickly when Elliot had appeared at the door of the cabin and afterwards Jem had little to say on the subject beyond complaining that the pony had near bitten his hand off when he attempted to stroke its nose.

The fact that the Indian had given the nugget as a gift to Jem did not surprise Elliot very much. Every once in a while an Indian – or a small group of Indians – would wander past the homestead. Generally, they were rootless people who had been separated from their tribes by war or the interference of whites or by a craving for drink. The Elliot homestead was about as far as they were inclined to penetrate into the realm of the white man and they were careful to avoid the town. Elliot was wary of them but Jem had no such inhibitions.

Elliot had gradually over the years learned to understand Jem's relationship with Indians and their attitude towards him. They recognized Jem's state of mind and knew that he was one who had been touched by the Great Spirit and was under His special protection. Most of them understood almost no English but would invariably stand and listen with an almost religious awe as Jem prattled on about ponies and toads and the harvest and what Chris had been saying and how Ma and Pa had died and the time he had seen a panther in the woods .... Then he would wave his wooden rifle about at random and show them how his Pa had carved it out and they would examine all its cuts and marks and listen to more of his meaningless words as if they were hearing the voice of the Great Spirit Himself. And sometimes they would give him little presents – a piece of calico, some tobacco or a bear's claw – almost as if they were making a gift to the spirits.

When he was younger, Elliot used to laugh at it all but he could not have laughed now. It seemed to him that Indian religion made as much sense as that of the Sunday School teachers or the Bible-thumping preachers with all their threats of hell fire and promises of heavenly bliss. If whites took all that so seriously it was amazing that they did not take more trouble to avoid the one and make tracks for the other! He had listened to plenty of preachers who had come out on to the battlefields after the fighting had finished to read a few words over the dead and to instruct the survivors that they must accept with humility the will of God, who, in His wisdom, had decided to take away the souls of their comrades – although it always seemed obvious to Elliot that they had been taken away by a bullet or by cannon fire or by a bayonet in the guts ....

The landscape had begun to open out as they approached that part of the valley in which their little farm lay. There were fewer trees and boulders and the grass stretched on all sides, rippling now in the faint breeze that stirred from the west. They had travelled about a mile or so further when the mule lifted up its ears and Elliot, with an almost instinctive reaction born of countless cavalry patrols, turned and looked back along the trail by which they had come.

In the distance, he saw a rider appearing over a crest in the ground and he knew at once by the black hat with its tiny flash of white and something about the set of the shoulders that it was the half-breed who had stood near to Wilson outside the saloon.

Elliot turned and looked straight ahead.

'Looks like we're being followed,' he grunted, half to himself.

'Yeah, I see'd him 'way long back,' replied Jem.

When he judged that the rider was within easy rifle range, Elliot gave the reins to Jem, turned around in the buggy and held his cavalry rifle ready in his hands. If this feller had any idea of taking revenge for his friend's humiliation and was planning to take a shot at them from the back, he would have to think again.

The rider seemed, however, to be undisturbed by Elliot's defensive posture and continued to gain upon them, his piebald pony moving at a steady trot. As he drew nearer, details of his appearance made themselves clear. He was a tall man, almost too large, it seemed, for his mount, and rode with the easy motion of long practice. Black hair hung down untidily under his black hat and he was dressed in a jacket and pants of buckskin, crumpled and greasy with long use. At his throat, the necklace that Elliot had caught sight of earlier turned out to be no Indian necklace but one made of fine silver, of the kind that a rich white woman might wear, and he wore high boots and spurs of an expensive southern pattern, now heavily coated with dust.

As he drew level with the buggy, the man slowed his pony to keep pace with the mule and turned his head, with just a hint of curiosity, towards Jem. His nose was large and his lips broad. What was most striking, however, was the pale colour of his eyes, contrasting with the dark complexion.

Jem returned his look and grinned. 'You a half-breed, mister?'

If the man felt any resentment at the bluntness of the question, he did not show it.

'Yeah, mother a full-blooded Blackfoot – father some kind of no-account trapper. Got hisself scalped as far as I know.'

He looked closely at Jem, then at Elliot, then back to Jem.

'You folks live hereabouts?'

Elliot spoke before Jem could. 'Who wants to know?'

'Name's Billy – Billy Wolf. Just passin' through,' he continued, seeming to anticipate Elliot's next question.

'Thought I saw you in the town.' Elliot frowned at the man's coolness which bordered on a kind of insolence. 'You got some kind of an interest in followin' this buggy?'

'Nope – just passin' by.'

The half-breed spurred his mount and drew away ahead, soon to pass over the horizon. Elliot kicked the mule into a quicker movement. It was obvious that the stranger could easily reach their deserted homestead before they did and he was disturbed at the thought. When they turned on to the stretch of trail, which led after about half a mile to their main gate, he searched the ground for signs that the rider had also turned into it but could see nothing. Not that that fact brought him any sense of relief. The half-breed was smart enough to skirt away round by the wooded slopes which overlooked the farm if he wished to observe without being seen. Elliot studiously avoided looking in that direction as he jumped down from the buggy and entered the house. He would just have given his own suspicions away and the man would take care not to show himself anyway.

'Here, Jem!' he shouted across the yard, as he always did. 'See to the mule and unload the stores, while I git somethin' ready for us to eat. I'm sure enough hungry!'

The next two days went by in the usual routine of hard work. Elliot thought from time to time about the incident with Wilson and his meeting with the half-breed but gradually it seemed to be unimportant. Wilson was just a loud mouth and maybe that half-Indian had no connection with him or with that Proctor feller. On the third morning, however, as he came out of the barn, he saw three mounted men coming up to the gate at a slow walk. The one at the front of the group was Proctor himself, who lifted his hand in a friendly gesture of greeting as he caught sight of Elliot. His two followers looked like a couple of out-of-work cowhands. All had guns at their belts and Elliot stiffened, realizing that, in the event of trouble, he had no chance of getting to his rifle which was in the house.

'Well, now, good mornin', Mr Elliot.' Proctor used the name as if he had always known it. 'Sure is nice to see you. We just thought we would drop by as somethin' important has come up. Need to ask you a couple of questions.'

His manner was ingratiating but there lurked behind it a suggestion of threat as if he was going to get some answers whether Elliot liked it or not.

'The fact is, there's been a man killed – prospector feller, by the name of Jones. Murdered up at the top o' this here valley.' He stopped speaking as if to study the effect of his words but Elliot gave no sign. 'We reckon he was killed by an Injun. Any Injuns pass this way lately?'

'Depends on what y'mean by "lately",' countered Elliot. He found it difficult to believe anything this man said. Everything about him prompted a distrust which went a long way back in Elliot. The man's air of superiority was of the sort cultivated by certain officers in the war who reckoned they were too smart and too damned important to get mixed up in the fighting themselves but were keen enough to send the troopers into the thick of it, regardless of the dangers. They were always the kind to take the full credit for things when they were going fine and ready to blame the men when it was going the other way.

Proctor scowled and then – as quickly – forced a smile again.

'Well, say last couple o' weeks or so .... Thing is, Mr Elliot, we got to catch this murderin' Injun. We can't let them redskins think that they kin get away with it or there's no tellin' what'll happen next.'

'Sounds like a job for the sheriff,' suggested Elliot, 'and maybe the Indian Agent.'

'Of course, we're bringin' the law into this as fast as we can but there's no time to be wasted. This goddam Injun's makin' his getaway right now!'

'You find the body of this prospector feller yourself?' asked Elliot.

'Two o' my men did. Bringing it in to the sheriff.'

'Must be kinda high, ain't it – after two weeks?'

Proctor looked at Elliot steadily.

'I didn't say that this man got killed two weeks since. I asked if you had seen any Injuns in that time. Fact is that this Injun has been keepin' company with Jones for a long time. Pretendin' to be a kind of friend, I suppose, till he saw his chance to murder the old feller and steal his gold. Anyhow, listen here, Elliot.' Proctor's tone was beginning to take on a hard edge. 'We intend finding this Injun and bringing him to justice and if you've got any sense, you'll help as much as you can. Now we know that an Injun called around here 'bout a week ago. We know that he spoke to that – brother o' yours. We want to speak to him. Ask him some questions.'

Elliot stared into Proctor's eyes as if he could read his mind. He knew that bringing any criminal to justice was the last thing that concerned him. This man, with his worn-out clothes that had been made for somebody else and riding a horse that its owner was still looking for – if he was still alive – was, in all probability, on the run from the law, himself. Nevertheless, the mention of the Indian visiting the homestead and the claim that he had stolen the gold worried Elliot.

'You ain't asking my brother no questions. He gets rattled and kinda mixed up when folks start badgerin' him. Anyhow, he don't know about any o' this.'

'I know about this brother o' yours. It's too bad that he ain't just right but that don't mean that he cain't tell us if that Injun said anythin' to him. This Injun ...' – he looked at Elliot closely as he spoke – 'calls himself Half Yeller Face. Cheyenne, so I heard tell.'

'What makes you think he came here?' asked Elliot.

'One of my men was on his trail but lost it up in the woods somewhere but then he looks down from that there hill and sees this Injun at your gate a'talkin' to your brother ....'

'I ain't much interested in what spyin' half-breed buzzards kin see from the hill!'

Elliot's anger drove through him, cold and sharp. He turned on his heel and walked quickly but with measured tread to the house. Fear for the trio of guns behind him had been swept from his mind. As he reached the doorway one of Proctor's men put a hand on his revolver but refrained from drawing at a signal from his boss.

Inside the house, Elliot picked up his rifle, loaded some shells and stepped back outside. The three men stared in surprise as he aimed it in their direction. The two down-beat cowhands flinched visibly but Proctor remained still.

'Time you and your men were on your way, Proctor.' Elliot's voice was steady and threatening. 'Your kind ain't welcome here. Better move out.'

'You're makin' a mistake, Elliot. You're settin' yourself agin the law.'

'If the sheriff wants to speak to me, I ain't goin' no place.'

'There's three of us here, Elliot, and just one o' you.'

Elliot had his rifle trained on Proctor's chest.

'Who's gonna take the first slug?'

They hesitated for a moment, then with an expression of anger and disgust, Proctor tugged his horse around and began to move off. Elliot watched them until they were out of sight, his anger gradually cooling and being replaced by a feeling of doubt.

It was hard to decide how much truth there was in the story that he had just heard. The part about the prospector being murdered was possible but unlikely. Elliot knew that mining had died out years ago in the region. At one time, way before the Civil War, when Elliot was just a kid, there had been some gold found in the hills and miners had flocked to the area but the seam, such as it was, had soon run out. Nobody had got rich out of it, as far as he knew, and pretty soon the last miner had gone, leaving nothing behind but abandoned, worked-out shafts and the rotting remains of their shacks. If some old prospector had been poking about there lately, it could only be because he had more optimism than sense.

Apart from that, the country for miles around the old

mines had now been designated by the government as an Indian reservation. Whites were discouraged from going there and any further activity in the mines would certainly not have been permitted. The government was anxious to settle the Indian population and was having enough trouble to get them to stay put on the reservation, which, as usual, was poor land, unfit for agriculture and with no game to speak of, and only available to the Indians because the whites could not think of a better use for it. The Indian Agent had his work cut out getting the co-operation that he needed to get the scheme to work and this old prospector, if he had ever existed, would have had to keep his head pretty low if he was going to avoid trouble with the Indians, the Agent or the government or all three combined.

Why would Proctor make up such a yarn? The simple answer might be that he had found out somehow that this Cheyenne, Half Yellow Face, did have some gold nuggets, which he had picked up somewhere or had stolen, and Proctor naturally, wanted them for himself. The talk about the murder and the law was aimed at getting the Elliots to tell him what they might have found out from that elusive Indian who had struck up a friendship with Jem.

Still, Proctor was right about the Indian having some gold. The nugget that he had given Jem was small but genuine. Maybe he had more and, who knows, maybe he had committed murder to get it.

Elliot turned and went back into the house, placing his rifle thoughtfully on the table where it would be within easy reach if Proctor should decide to make another visit within the next hour or so. He had better have another talk with Jem.

'Chris! Hey, Chris!' Jem came hurrying across the yard from the stable, shovel in hand. 'Who were those fellers, Chris? What did they want?'

'They was lookin' for somebody. Say, Jem, that Injun

who gave you the gold nugget, did he say anythin' that you maybe forgot to tell me? He say anythin' about a prospector? Feller called Jones?'

Jem looked thoughtful, chin in hand.

'Nope.' He shook his head slowly. 'He didn't say nothin' about nobody called Jones. Who the tarnation is Jones? He one o' these fellers jest rode away?'

Elliot questioned his brother patiently, almost without appearing to do so. Getting information from Jem was like fishing for roach with a little bit of wool on your hook instead of a worm – you would be damn lucky if you came up with anything. This time there didn't seem to be any more fish to catch. There was just the pony that had darned near bit him, the nugget and the Injun with the funny name ....

'OK, Jem, it don't matter. But listen, what did ya do with that nugget? You put it in the ginger jar, like I said?'

Jem looked into the fireplace, then at the ceiling, then out of the window, his face a picture of childish guilt.

'Well, no, I got it here in my pocket. I put it in the jar then I took it out to look at it. I forgot.'

'Well, you go right now and put it back in the jar. We gotta keep it safe.'

Elliot hardly heard the tiny nugget clink to the bottom of his mother's old ginger jar, that still stood above the fireplace. His mind remained troubled. Should he ride into town to tell the sheriff what he had heard? This Proctor feller must have known something about all of this when he was in town the other day otherwise his entire attitude towards the incident with Wilson and Elliot would have been different. Even then he had been interested in gaining the confidence of Elliot so as to find out what information, if any, Jem could come out with. So the whole story of the murder must have been in his mind but he had not reported it to the sheriff. Was this because it was all a lie or was there more to it than that?

Even as he turned the idea over in his mind Elliot knew that he would not ride into town. Not yet anyway. He could not leave the place deserted while Proctor and his gang were still in the neighbourhood. What might he come back to? Nor could he leave Jem on his own. That would be the most dangerous thing of all. Best just to do nothing but to keep looking over his shoulder. Let Proctor make the next move if he had a mind to. He, Elliot, would be ready.

TWO

Billy Wolf sighed as he crouched among the rocks and the scrub of the hillside and peered through the tops of the trees on to the Elliot place below. This kind of job always tried his patience. For the last couple of days he had spent a lot of time up here, keeping an eye on the farm in case anybody decided to go off into the town and to let Proctor know if they did. He, Billy, didn't know what all the pussy-footin' about was for. His way would just have been to bring down the cavalry feller with a slug in the leg or somewheres where it wouldn't kill him right off and then move in with the boys and beat the hell out of him and his loopy brother until they told Proctor where the gold was – if they knew – or until it became pretty obvious that they didn't. But Proctor, although he wasn't against violence, seemed to think that there was sometimes better ways of doing things, though Billy wasn't all that sure what they were. Proctor wasn't lookin' to fall foul of the law right now, o' course, not until they had had a real good chance to scout around for that gold but the way things were, it didn't look as if it was goin' to work out that way ....

Right now, the Elliots were workin' in the barn where they had spent most of their time lately, pilin' up the hay or somethin', and didn't show any sign of goin' anywheres but Proctor had told him to keep checkin' on the place with this goddamned telescope that Proctor had picked up with a few other things during the war, just about the time when he had to jump the army because it looked as though they was fixin' to court martial him for rape and pillage.

Trouble was that this kind of job always set Billy to thinking and he wasn't too fond of that. There was no way of stopping his mind from drifting way back to the start when he was just a kid being dragged around by his Blackfoot mother and some other Injuns somewhere around the foothills of the Rocky Mountains, when they had all been trainin' him to be a real good Injun and to hate the whites. What had happened to his mother he couldn't ever remember, but the next thing he knew, he was in the Mission with a few other stray Injun kids and a couple of white orphans where they were supposed to be learning how to read and write and to know about the Bible, but the Injun kids there kept callin' him a no-account half-breed and the white kids said the same, and one of the bigger white boys used to punch and kick him whenever they had the time for a bit of recreation in between Bible readings. This boy had told the father that Billy had stolen a lump of boiled ham that the father had been keeping for himself and Billy had taken a real good thrashin', although the truth was that he had no idea what boiled ham tasted like.

He reckoned, though, that it must have been then that his Blackfoot blood had really taken over because when that white boy had come out to the latrines at the edge of the Mission about sundown, he had got the biggest and last surprise of his life when he had felt Billy's arm around his throat and about four inches of rusty old Bowie knife being shoved in between his shoulder blades.

After that, Billy had gone on the run, picking up this and that, and wonderin' whether to try to find his way back to the Blackfeet or to try to be a white man. In the end he had decided that he might do better to try to be a white since they generally got the best of everything and were always pushing the Injuns around. So he had spent two-three years going around workin' for the whites –

real swell jobs too, like shovelling manure on the farms and cleanin' up the spit in the saloons – but even at that they couldn't let him ever forget who he was and one thing he noticed was that the more respectable and God-fearin' they were, the more convinced they seemed to be that a low-down, no-account half-breed like him hardly had no right to live never mind stinkin' up the neighbourhood near decent Christian folks like themselves ….

So then Billy had started to do a bit of thieving – not much, just a bit of extra food here and there and the few dollars that folks were inclined to leave carelessly lyin' around in their pockets – and then he stole a gun and used it to empty a storekeeper out of the saddle and had gone off with the horse and his gun and what money the storekeeper had had with him, to make a start on his new career. And for a while he had done pretty good too, like the time he had met the Texas rancher who used to wear the fancy boots, but then things hadn't been going quite so well for a few years and since taking up with Proctor and his gang he hadn't exactly been makin' his fortune ….

Billy roused himself from his reverie and put the glass again to his eye, scanning the tiny farmstead below for signs of change. The cavalry feller was still in the barn but his loopy brother was just going into the house, maybe to make some coffee or something, which was just about what Billy could have done with right now. Billy sat back, scratching the back of his neck. That loopy kid was lucky to be alive after callin' him a half-breed like that. Billy had been in two minds whether to let him have a bullet in the guts but Proctor had said that he was to try to find out what he could by bein' kind of friendly and gainin' the loopy feller's confidence but that irritable brother of his, who still seemed to think he was in the Civil War, had sat there on the buckboard with his finger itching on the trigger of that army rifle and all set to discourage friendly conversation.

That gopher was always on the look-out for trouble. Couple of times Billy had seen him through the telescope, standing just inside the barn door, looking up at the hill as if he thought that somebody might be spying on him. But Billy was confident that his hiding place was well chosen. He wasn't half Blackfoot for nothin', after all ....

Something was going on, though, down there .... The loopy feller had come out of the back door of the house and was standin' in the yard, wavin' that crazy wooden gun of his around as if he was fixin' to shoot somethin'. Now he was walking over to the paddock, which the dappled horse shared with the old mule, climbed the gate and was walking more quickly now to the far fence as if he was getting all excited. Now he was over the outside fence and was hurrying through the long grass to the edge of the woods.

Whatever the loopy kid was doin', Billy was sure that his brother did not know about it. That cavalry feller had been real suspicious ever since Proctor had decided on that fool idea of ridin' up to that place with his two hill-billies as if he thought he was the sheriff or somethin'. That was the dumbest fool thing that had come out of all this yet! It had really put that feller on his guard. He sure wasn't goin' to let his kid brother wander off the homestead for a long time to come.

But there it was happenin' ... the cavalry feller was still workin' in the barn, wonderin' when the hell the coffee was goin' to be ready, while his damn fool brother was takin' to the woods ....

Billy slid back with practised caution until he judged it safe to stand up. This might just be a chance. Proctor hadn't told him to do anything except just report back but if they were all going to sit around waiting for Proctor to make all the decisions, they would still be here in the winter snows.

He moved quickly and quietly back through the scrub and boulders to the spot where he had left his pony. If

Loopy stayed in the woods long enough it should be possible to get close to him without too much trouble. Billy mounted swiftly and began riding downhill, circling around in the hope of reaching that part of the woods where he guessed Jem might be if he kept up the direction and pace he had started off with. After a time, the slope eased off and he found himself entering into the woods where he was forced to slow down and advance with caution.

The woods were silent except for the faint rustle of leaves. Once in a while, a songbird would flutter overhead, chirping out its defiance of him as he pressed his reluctant pony deeper into the threatening shade. For a lengthy period, he was almost convinced that he had miscalculated or that Jem had turned back to the farm, then he heard a voice fairly close to hand which seemed raised in argument. Billy stopped, feeling that the opportunity had slipped away if Jem had met up with somebody else, but then another thought struck him and he slipped off his pony's back and crept forward on foot. He heard the voice again and this time he saw Jem standing nearby a fallen log, pointing his wooden gun downwards at something that Billy could not yet see.

'I got ya this time! This time you're comin' back with me. No use tryin' to hide neither. I knew I would get ya this time!'

Mystified, Billy moved forward slowly and silently until he was in a position behind Jem and realized that he was directing his remarks at a large green and yellow frog, which sat on the opposite side of a small pool which had formed, after the recent rains, in the hollow created by the tearing up of the tree's roots as it had fallen during some past storm. Billy shook his head in silent wonder and then stood up.

'Surely you ain't gonna shoot that dumb critter with that there rifle. It ain't done you no harm, has it?'

Jem turned slowly, with a broad grin, but showed no surprise at the interruption.

'Hey, you're the half-breed feller, ain't ya?'

Billy sucked in his breath.

'Yeah, you could say that – but not too many more times .... But how come a big feller like you is still playin' around with a kid's wooden gun? Ain't you got a real rifle?'

'Well, no, we ain't got more than one gun at home and Chris won't never let me touch it.'

'Well, now, that's too bad ... big feller like you too. What age are you anyways?'

'Well, about twenty, I guess,' said Jem, uncertainly.

'Seems to me a growed-up feller like you oughta have his own rifle. You just come along with me and I'll fix you up real good with the smartest rifle you ever did see!'

'Yeah?' Jem looked at him incredulously. 'But how come ...?'

'I got two, three rifles back there.' Billy waved vaguely up the wooded hillside. 'I cain't use more than one at a time. You come along with me and I'll give one to ya, sure as hell.'

He put an arm around Jem's shoulder and began to lead him gently but firmly back the way he had come and towards the spot where his pony awaited him.

After a few yards, Jem suddenly stopped in his tracks.

'Yeah, but listen, I cain't go away from the farm. Chris told me straight. He would be real mad if he knew I had come into the woods after that old frog. I got to go back.'

Billy looked at him closely, trying to size up his state of mind. He had already decided that cajolery and threats would do no good when dealing with a guy like this. He was also aware that, by this time, Elliot would have missed his brother and would be searching around for him. If shooting was to be avoided, like Proctor said, then they had to move fast but quiet.

'Listen, I had a word with Chris. When you was in the house. When ya went in to make coffee or somethin'.'

'Jeez, the coffee ... I forgot.'

'Well, it don't matter about the coffee.' Billy was conscious of speaking in a low voice, fearful that Elliot might already be within earshot. 'Chris says that ya really oughta have your own rifle by this time. He says he'll be mighty pleased if I was to give ya a real smart repeater rifle that ya could keep all to yourself an' ya could go huntin' with and shoot deer and bears and whatever the hell you liked. But we gotta go quick. We ain't got too much time. I got work to do. We gotta hurry.'

They went off at a more rapid pace, Jem's face beaming with delight at the thought of the glittering prize before him, Billy with a sense of rising impatience. When they reached the pony, Billy persuaded his companion to mount up behind him, and spurred the animal into a trot in spite of its double load.

After about an hour of increasingly uncomfortable riding, during which Jem almost fell off more than once, and the rain, which had been threatening all day, began to come down heavily, adding to the general discomfort, they had left the woods well behind them and were making their way slowly through an area of rock and scree. Ahead of them the land was gradually rising towards the rugged hills which hung dark and wet against the background of low cloud.

'When the hell are we gonna stop?' complained Jem, for the twentieth time. 'I gotta git back to Chris!'

'It's OK about Chris,' grunted Billy. 'You jest hold on – we's nearly there ....'

'Where the tarnation are we goin' anyways?' demanded Jem, in whose mind the thought of the rifle had been replaced by a desire to get back to the comfort of the kitchen stove.

Billy did not answer but urged his mount into a slightly faster walk and after a further lengthy period of plodding, during which Jem slumped forward as if to protect himself from the lashing rain which had already soaked him through, they rounded an outcrop of rock and found themselves within a few yards of a rough camp. This consisted of two hastily erected tents made of old canvas and a small fire, placed partly under the shelter of the overhanging rock. Some distance beyond the bivouac tents stood a group of tethered horses, miserable in the wet. The fire smoked and flickered fitfully, scarcely warming the blackened coffee pot which stood in its embers. Beside the fire were two men, heads and shoulders covered by dirty horse-blankets. They turned as they heard the pony on the gravelly track and both gaped in astonishment.

'Gawd, here's Billy bringin' in that goofy kid!' yelled Wilson.

Billy Wolf allowed his exhausted pony to come to a halt. He wiped some of the rain from his nose and mouth and scowled down at them.

'You gophers sure keep a real smart look-out,' he said, with heavy sarcasm. 'Thought there was supposed to be some hog's-bladder posted halfways down thet trail in case I had any messages or anythin'!'

'Wilson was supposed to do thet,' smirked the short, heavily-set man with the scar on his forehead, who stood looking with curiosity at Billy's passenger, 'but he don't like the rain.'

'I had ta come back for somethin' to wear 'gainst this wet,' growled Wilson, defensively. 'I ain't a goddam muskrat!'

'Ya coulda fooled me,' answered Billy. He twisted around in the saddle and slapped Jem on the shoulder. 'Here ya kin git down now. We's here.'

Jem half slid – half fell to the ground and stood looking about with the uncomprehending air of a sleepwalker who has just awakened in strange surroundings.

'Here, I gotta git back to Chris ....'

They had been joined by Proctor and three other men who had come out of the bivouacs on hearing Wilson's yell. Proctor stared almost in disbelief at Billy Wolf.

'I didn't exactly tell ya to bring him in,' he complained. 'I says to keep a look out for Elliot goin' into town or somewheres and leavin' the kid so thet I could git a chance to ask him a few questions. Nobody asked for no kidnappin'.'

'I didn't exactly kidnap him – just a bit o' persuasion and you kin ask him questions just as easy here ....'

Proctor frowned thoughtfully.

'What about Elliot? Where's he right now?'

Billy grinned on his way to the coffee pot.

'Expect he's on his way up here – mad as hell.'

Proctor shook his head. If there was one thing you could nearly always depend upon with Billy Wolf it was that he would do what he hadn't been asked ....

'All right!' His voice took on a note of command. 'Wilson and Biss – you two git down that trail a good long ways and keep your eyes skinned for Elliot. If he's gonna come up here shootin' we'd better be ready for him. But no shootin', remember, unless he starts it and if you kin git the drop on him, take him in too. May as well round up the whole family, now thet we've started!'

The two men mounted reluctantly and set off down the track by which Billy and his captive had just arrived.

'It's a sure thing,' muttered Wilson, under his breath, 'that, if I git the drop on Elliot, I won't be takin' no prisoners ....'

Proctor turned his attention to Jem, who stood still in the pouring rain, looking mystified and dejected. He put an arm protectively around the young man's shoulder and began to steer him towards the nearest tent.

'Come on, son, you're wet through. Better git yourself dried out. Here, Pulley, help Jem off wi' these wet clothes and git them dried at the fire – and git him a mug o' coffee while you're about it. We gotta look after him. Don't want ya gittin' numonay, son, do we?'

'What in hell do ya think I am – a goddamned nursemaid?' growled Pulley. But he did what he was told and helped Jem off with his wet shirt and pants and set them up on a stick to dry in the smoke of the fire.

As Jem sat in the bivouac, with an Indian blanket around his shoulders, sipping coffee and looking utterly lost, Proctor studied him, wondering where to begin. This kid was simple-minded, no doubt about that, but he knew something about that gold and Proctor was determined to find out what it was. That Indian had not stopped at the Elliot place and spoken to this feller for no reason. After all, the Cheyenne must have realized that he was being trailed after he met up with Proctor and his gang, and he was putting himself in some added danger by wasting time when he should have been making all speed to get well away. He had stopped because he wanted to tell these Elliots something important and it was obvious to Proctor that it could only have been about the gold – unless he had spoken about the murder of Jones – but Proctor felt certain that the Elliots had not known about that before he had told them himself that day he rode up with Pulley and Haze. He had watched Elliot's face like a hawk all the time they had been speaking and he was sure that Elliot had never heard of Jones or the murder. The gold, he wasn't quite so sure about. He thought he had noticed a wary look come into the feller's eyes when he had mentioned the word – but, even then, he wasn't too certain ....

That was why he had decided to pick on the kid brother for answering the questions. According to Billy Wolf, the Cheyenne had only spoken to the kid – so he must know at least as much as his brother. Also, of course, being simple-minded, as everybody in Red Creek had confirmed, he probably wouldn't have enough sense to keep his mouth shut – if he was asked in the right way. His brother would have been a different kettle of fish altogether. Proctor had met men like Elliot before, stiff-necked, stubborn, suspicious, awkward characters; fellers who were as tough as smoked buffalo hide and would hardly give you the time of day without charging five cents. Even at the point of a gun, Elliot would be hard to get anything out of – especially when he knew that he was worth more alive than dead.

'Here, Jem, how ya feelin' now?' Proctor searched in his mind for an opening gambit. 'Hey, that's sure some swell farm thet you two have over there! Bet you and Chris get on real well too. Real fine feller that Chris.'

Jem looked up with a little spark of interest and gradually, under Proctor's cheerful sounding remarks and friendly attitude, began to open up a bit about the farm and his life with Chris. To Proctor, it all sounded confused and childish as Jem's conversation, because of his inability to concentrate on a topic for more than a few moments, tended to sound incoherent. After listening with as much patience as he could muster, for what seemed an age, he managed gradually to turn Jem's mind in the direction of the all-important meeting with the Cheyenne. However, even after he had succeeded in doing this he was disappointed, as Jem's account centred around the pony which had almost bitten him and contained nothing else that seemed to make any sense.

Eventually, Proctor sat back in silence, inwardly cursing and curbing his desire to smack this fool of a boy across the ear. He had always known that the kid was simple-minded but he had never thought that he would be quite as dumb as this! There did not seem to be any way of getting anything out of him. Either he had never known anything or he had totally forgotten it. If that goddam Cheyenne had said anything about the gold it must have gone in one ear and straight out the other.

However, he had better give it another try. This half-witted boy was all that they had left to go on. The Cheyenne had been too damn smart for Billy Wolf and had given him the slip by doubling back on the trail or covering up his tracks in some cunning Indian way. Proctor had thought that he might be heading for the reservation but Billy had said no – that reservation was packed with maybe three or four hundred Absarokee and the Absarokee and the Cheyenne Indians hadn't been on speaking terms for a long, long time. That Cheyenne, if he had any sense, was high-tailing it for the Black Hills by this time.

Problem was, though, was he high-tailing it with the gold or without it? As far as they had been able to tell from his tracks after they first got on to him, he had not picked up any gold or anything else from a hiding place along the way but maybe after they had lost him he had managed to do just that.

There were times when he felt like shooting that trigger-happy half-breed! There hadn't been any good reason for putting a bullet into that old prospector when they came across his camp away up the valley. When the gang had arrived by chance upon him that evening, the old man had been real scared and had told them he was on his way down to the nearest town as he had turned sick and wanted to see a doctor. He had had a little rawhide bag with him with about three gold nuggets in it and was all set to hand it over, real peaceable, but Billy had shot him just the same – more or less out of force of habit and then the old man had begun screaming and groaning and shouting out for his friend, Half Yeller Face, and promising that if they would only get him a doctor so as not to let him die, he and his Indian pal would show them where the gold was hidden – plenty of gold, a whole big bag full .... Then Wilson had started to hit him around the face so as to get more information out of him without getting in any doctor, the nearest one being about a day's ride down the valley anyway, but then the old goat had fallen back with his mouth wide open and full of blood and that had been the end of him.

So they had all stood around cursing for a while because they reckoned they had missed a really good chance of becoming rich and blaming Billy for being too hasty as they felt quite sure that the old man would have told them anything they wanted to know rather than take a bullet.

It was then that Billy Wolf had heard a faint sound in the trees nearby and they had all turned just in time to see an Indian standing there with a look of amazement on his face which had changed to an expression which reminded Proctor of an enraged cougar, trying to make up its mind to spring. But the sight of all the guns had made him think better of it and he had vanished into the gathering shadows as silently as he had come. It had been too late to get on his trail that night but next morning they had, but pretty soon they lost it and had to fan out in the hope of picking it up again. They had no luck with that, though, and the last sighting they had of that Indian was when Billy had spotted him at the Elliots' place.

'Hey, boss, take a look at this!' Pulley was leaning into the tent, his face lit up with excitement. In his hand he held a tiny gold nugget. 'Fell out the kid's shirt pocket!'

Proctor's eyes opened wide as he snatched it from the man's palm. This was it! – this must mean something! He turned to Jem, forcing himself to speak in a calm tone.

'Say, Jem, where did ya get this? Looks like a gold nugget.'

'Oh, Gawd.' Jem put his hand to his forehead as if distraught. 'I shoulda put that back in the ginger jar! I forgot again! Chris will be real mad at me ....'

'This nugget belong to Chris?'

'Well, kind of. Injun gave it to me. Half Yeller Face.'

Proctor looked at him in silence, his mind busy. So that goddamned Cheyenne did have gold with him all along. Quite likely he had it all and was laughing all the way back to the Black Hills! He swore under his breath.

'That son-of-a-bitch. See if I could get to him ....'

'Yeah, son-of-a ....' Jem seemed to be searching in his mind for something almost entirely forgotten. 'Son-of-a – sun – sun-stones.' He grinned suddenly and said to nobody in particular, 'Sun-stones up in Dead Mouth.'

Proctor stared at him blankly. What in hell was the fool ravin' about now? Jem continued to talk to himself.

'Half Yeller Face,' he chortled again at the name. 'He was sayin' about them sun-stones up in Dead Mouth.'

Proctor reached out and grabbed him by the shoulder as if in a desperate attempt to hold on to a dear friend who has fallen into the frozen lake and is in imminent danger of disappearing under the ice.

'What did he mean, Jem? What was it he meant?'

But the ice had closed over Jem's memory. There was nothing else – just the sun-stones, Dead Mouth and the ill-tempered pony with the sharp teeth.

Proctor got up, feeling his temper rising, and stalked out of the tent. Billy Wolf was poking at the fire in an effort to stir up enough heat to give him a warm cup of coffee. In one hand he held Jem's wooden rifle, which he was examining with mild curiosity. He looked up at Proctor's approach.

'Better give this back to the kid,' he grunted.

'Sling it into the fire,' growled Proctor. 'Goddamned fool ....'

Surprisingly, Billy did not do so, but walked over to the tent and threw it in, where Jem clutched it, as a child with a toy.

'Listen, Billy,' – Proctor was tense – 'you ever heard o' "sun-stones"?'

'Sure, just another name for gold nuggets. Some Indians call them that.'

'That's what I was beginning to think,' nodded Proctor. 'You ever heard o' Dead Mouth? Maybe some place called Dead Mouth ...?'

Billy looked thoughtful.

'Yeah, some guys in the saloon said somethin' about it. You remember ya said to ask around a bit about gold minin' in these parts. I already told ya. They said the gold was all cleared out years ago.'

'I remember ya said that.'

'Well, some of them was speaking about mines like Birch Falls, Blue Top, Dead Mouth.'

'That's it. That's where the gold came from.' Proctor held out the nugget under Billy's nose. 'That blasted Cheyenne had this with him – maybe all the rest too.'

Billy shook his head.

'Don't reckon so. That old prospector was makin' his way into town to get a doctor because he was sick. He wouldn'ta carried all that gold with him. Would make more sense to cache it some place till he felt fit enough to come back to collect it. Seems to me that if that gold ain't still in the place it started out in, then it's way up the valley somewhere, in some hidin' place where the old man stuck it before he set out.'

Proctor weighed it all up in his mind. It seemed to make sense and there was a chance that the gold was hidden in this Dead Mouth mine or nearby. It was far and away the best lead they had had all along.

'That's where we're goin',' he said simply.

Billy looked at him closely.

'All them old mines is in the Injun reservation. Whole goddamned country around is crawlin' with Absarokee. Could be we won't be too welcome.'

Proctor hesitated. He had tangled with Indians before and preferred to keep well clear of them – at least when there was a whole bunch. One lousy Cheyenne was a different matter. Still there was too much at stake and there were seven of them and all well armed. There might not be too much trouble. He felt that he had to take the risk.

'We'll go anyway. First thing in the mornin'. Too late to start out now.'

'What about the kid?'

Proctor looked at Billy sharply. It was unlike Billy Wolf to concern himself with such details.

'We'll take him along,' he answered. 'Could be he'll remember somethin' else on the way.'

Billy nodded. 'Tell ya another thing. That kid's plumb

loco.' He grinned at Proctor's rueful expression. 'He's a Crazy Man. That don't mean nothin' to you and me but to the Injuns, it means somethin' kinda special – he's in touch with the Great Spirit. Got special protection, see, and when they see him in our company, they might just have a different attitude. Might even be friendly to us, if we don't get them all riled up by messin' around too much on their territory.'

'Hope you're right but we'll blast them to hell if we have to.'

Billy grinned again.

'We might have to.'

They set off next day under a heavy dawn sky, the rain still falling in a steady drizzle. They were cold and wet but inspired at the thought of the possible riches ahead of them. Proctor rode at the head, his eyes narrowed in deep thought. The rest followed in loose formation, with Haze keeping a look-out at the rear. Elliot had not shown up yesterday but there was always the chance that he would. Jem sat sulkily on a spare horse, watched over by Billy Wolf, and with his mind full of resentment and worry. Proctor had told him that they were heading for some place where they would meet Chris but he found it hard to believe and he hadn't even been given his new rifle ....

A little way back, Wilson rode silently, bitterly regretting that he hadn't had the chance the day before to put a slug into Elliot, his angry eyes lingering from time to time on the crazy kid.

THREE

Elliot stood stock still, rifle in hand, his eyes riveted upon the footprint which marked itself out, from its depth and shape, from the confused mass of other prints which surrounded it in the mud around the little pool. He knew beyond doubt that it had been made by a high boot of Mexican or Texas pattern and, as the realization came to him, his heart sank.

So he had been right all along that they were being watched from the hill by that half-breed .... He had always felt it although he had seen no actual sign of it until now. And the low, spying rat had seen Jem wandering from the farm and had raced down here to meet him.

Elliot shook his head, cursing himself for a fool. He ought to have known that Jem could not be trusted to remember that he had been told not to leave the farm, even if he was only playing around in the nearby woods as he often did. Elliot had followed his tracks easily enough across the paddock and through the grass to the trees but then he had lost them amid all Jem's tracks, old and new, which mazed in all directions. So then he had gone to the places which he knew were Jem's favourites; the rabbit warren, the broken down old elm where the long-eared owl nested every year and, at length, the little pool by the fallen birch. As he went, he had called out Jem's name several times but now there was need for silence.

Controlling his anxiety and rising temper only with

difficulty, he followed the tracks up through the woods, his rifle at the ready, eyes and ears alert. The trail of the two was easy to follow and every few yards he saw clearly the mark of a sharp heel. At last he came to a spot where a horse had stood waiting for some time and he knew that they had mounted up there and he had little chance of overtaking them on foot, even if the animal was overburdened.

He turned then and ran downhill, through the grasping branches, stumbling here and there in the undergrowth, until he was back home. Within minutes he had rounded up and saddled his dappled horse and was riding out, skirting the deeper part of the woods until he arrived once again near the place where the half-breed's pony had waited. As he reached it, however, the rain began to fall more and more heavily so that he groaned inwardly in the knowledge that the tracks might soon be lost.

Nevertheless, he followed them as far as he was able until they petered out on the scoured rock and in the rainwater which trickled and flooded downhill. All around, the landscape was rugged with strewn boulders and escarpments of granite through which he had to pick his way with difficulty. The light was fading also and he knew that he could do no more until morning. By then God knows what would have become of Jem. It was obvious that he had been taken in the hope of getting some information from him about Jones and the gold or something he had learned from the Cheyenne Indian. It was information that Elliot felt sure his brother did not have and would have the greatest difficulty in remembering even if he had been told of it. How would Proctor and his gang set about obtaining information from Jem? Elliot felt pretty sure that he knew the answer to that and he turned cold at the thought.

There was nothing for it now, though, except to turn back and to make his way with the utmost care through

the dusk and the slippery scree and pebbles in the
direction of the homestead. Soon he was forced to
dismount for the safety of his horse and to lead her at a
slow walk.

On his way, his mind was a turmoil of emotion;
dismay and anger, frustration and hatred, through
which calm, reasoned thought emerged only after an
hour of plodding through the darkness and rain.
Should he go into town in the hope of getting some help
from the law? The idea scarcely came into his mind than
it was dismissed. He knew Mulligan, the sheriff, and was
well aware of the kind of man he was. Elliot could well
imagine how he would react if he was asked to help in
this. Complacent in his own inertia, he would think of
every possible excuse to do nothing, especially if he
thought that there might be danger in the offing. He
would never have heard of Proctor or his gang or of
Jones or any murder and if the Elliot boy wanted to go
off with some stranger what could he be expected to do
about it? He wasn't a nursemaid and what evidence was
there that the boy hadn't gone off willingly? How did
Elliot know he had been kidnapped? And if Elliot had
thought that there had been anything in this yarn about
some old prospector being murdered, why had he not
reported it to him, the sheriff, at the time, instead of
waiting two-three days until his kid brother got mixed
up in it? Anyway, what the hell, he was a busy man, he
couldn't go riding all over the territory after every
goddamned rumour that came in ....

No, there was no help to be got from the law, not as it
existed at Red Creek at any rate. This was something
that he, himself, had to deal with. He had known that all
along and deep within his heart he was aware that he
would have had to deal with it himself in any case,
regardless of the kind of sheriff who sat in that office in
Red Creek. He would have taken help from anyone in
order to save Jem, but there was something held in
reserve, in the depth of his being, which demanded that

he must mete out justice or revenge, or whatever else it came to be known as, at the end of the encounter which was looming up ahead, like the battles he had known before and sometimes still dreamed of ....

When he reached home, he put his horse into the stable, grooming and feeding her as usual and then set about preparing himself for the journey in the morning. He dried off his clothes in front of the stove and brought out the waterproof cape which had remained with him from his cavalry service. He checked his rifle and ammunition and packed his saddle-bag with dried meat, biscuit and coffee. After that, he sat for a long time in deep thought before he lay down on his bunk to get what sleep he could.

At dawn, the rain was still falling but he saddled up early and set off, his mind already clear as to his plan of campaign – such as it was. He would follow the trail he had taken last night and then go further on in the same general direction for a time, in the hope of seeing some sign which he could not have seen in the fading light of the previous attempt. If that failed, as he believed it probably would, he had in his mind one or two places where the gang might have decided to spend a wet night, assuming they were still within a few miles of the farm. If he failed in this, and could not pick up their tracks by moving around in ever-widening circles, then he would follow up his last hope which was that they would cross the valley and ride towards the old mining area. What these men were after was gold – gold dug up and maybe hidden by that old prospector and it seemed to Elliot that it might just still be somewhere around there and that, in the end, that was the place where they would look for it. Whether Jem would still be alive then was another matter but maybe he would be. They had no reason for killing the boy so maybe they wouldn't. It was a slim chance but it seemed all that he had.

So he began his long exhausting search through the rain and over the rough ground. By the afternoon, he realized that it had all been in vain. There were no tracks to be found and no sign of an encampment in any of the places in which he searched. He changed his route and journeyed by degrees down towards the valley floor, his eyes continually searching the ground for the faintest trace of a hoof-print or scree kicked up by the passage of a horse or a stone dislodged by some force other than the weather. Also, he kept scanning the horizon of huge boulders and crags, interspersed by coarse grass and bushes and stunted trees, for any movement that would give him warning of danger. From time to time, he crossed small streams which were tributaries of the Calfskin River, which ran the full length of the valley, eventually meandering past Red Creek and on to the flat plains beyond.

As he descended, the grasses became more lush and the clumps of trees healthier and richer in appearance. The weather slowly improved until the last of the clouds vanished as wisps of cirrus in the wind that blew high overhead towards the distant mountaintops. In other circumstances, his mind would have been uplifted by the beauty of his surroundings, but the change brought no flicker of response from the leaden weight of his inner being except a rising hope that the dryer conditions would enable him to pick up some trace of the men who had become vipers in his mind, to be stamped mercilessly out of existence.

Towards late afternoon, he found himself on the banks of the Calfskin and was forced to ride some miles downstream to reach the ford which he had known since boyhood but had not visited for some years. Here the crossing was easy, the river having broadened out enough to be shallow on its firm pebbly bed and Elliot walked his horse over with slow confidence. On the other side was the inner edge of an ox-bow bend, consisting of flat sandy ground mixed with gravel and only sparsely populated by reeds and bulrushes. Here he stopped suddenly, his brain prompted into alertness at the sight of the tracks ahead of him.

It looked as though a party of horsemen had come past this spot only hours since. There seemed to have been three horses and they had not crossed at the ford but had travelled downstream on the opposite side from the route taken by Elliot. His heart leapt at the thought that Jem might have ridden one of the animals and had passed this way so recently. His captors could have crossed the Calfskin at some point much further up the valley and have followed the course of the river as a comparatively easy trail on their way to the valley floor. The fact that there seemed to be only two other horsemen with Jem was not so very surprising. The others – how many there were, Elliot did not know – might well be camped much further on … maybe well on the way to the old mining region.

Elliot pushed on as quickly as he thought was good for his tiring horse and found the tracks easy to follow. Within a half-mile or so, they left the river bank and began leading across the valley towards the hills. Elliot felt his spirits rising at this evidence that he had guessed correctly and that the horsemen ahead were members of Proctor's gang on their way to the mines and still to meet up with their main party. If he could overtake them within the next few hours, he might have only these two guards to deal with, which would give him a fighting chance of overcoming them – especially if he had the element of surprise – and rescuing his brother. One of them might even be that half-breed! He could not be sure from the tracks whether or not one of the mounts ahead was the Indian pony that he had seen him on before, or whether the man might have changed to another horse, but if he was there, and if anything had happened to Jem, that half-breed would be the first to suffer!

The tracks were leading in approximately the direction he had intended taking, towards the distant hills, and it was evident from the pace of the horses that their riders were in no hurry. After a time, that fact began to sow a seed of doubt in his mind. Men in their situation would be more likely to push on. They would be, to some extent, excited by events, and there was the rest of the gang to meet up with and the prospect of gold somewhere up ahead. They might allow their horses some respite but they would not dawdle – not for mile after mile ...

The question that had arisen in his mind was answered more swiftly than he had anticipated. The first sign that he was about to come upon the party he had been following was a trace of smoke hanging in the air just over the crest of the next rise. He halted warily and then advanced with the greatest caution. He was about to slip from his horse's back to reconnoitre on foot, when he caught a glimpse of a figure which appeared in view for a brief moment and then, as quickly, vanished. In that moment, however, he knew that there was a woman there – a young woman with black hair and wearing a bright red jacket.

Elliot sighed, his disappointment showing in his face, and spurred his horse into a trot. Within minutes he had arrived at the scene of the temporary camp. There was a small fire there, attended to by a greying man with sharp features and a gun at his belt. There were three horses, one of them a pack animal laden with tents and other gear. A groundsheet was spread out, upon which stood a neat little basket, of the kind a lady might take out for a picnic. The girl was seated, evidently about to partake of some refreshment. As Elliot approached, she pretended not to have seen him until he brought his mount to a standstill a few yards from her.

'Good day, ma'am,' the words of common courtesy came from his lips in a stumbling grunt. If he could have made a wide detour to avoid the meeting, he would have taken it but he had known from his first sight of her that she had seen him in the short distance and would have thought him a fool for being too diffident, as she would have interpreted his motive, to approach her.

'Oh, good day to you too, Mr Elliot.' Her eyes, deep brown in colour, sparkled with amusement.

He was faintly surprised that she remembered his name, although the population of Red Creek and the surrounding valley was so small that only complete strangers to the region went unrecognized. He had seen her from time to time in the town and knew that she was Julie Campbell, daughter of the Indian Agent, who lived on a prosperous spread some miles downriver.

'Such a pleasant day to go out riding, Mr Elliot.' Her words almost bordered on sarcasm as she took in his rough, travel-worn appearance, his unshaven face, his tired eyes. 'But,' her tone changed to one of polite concern, 'I feel sure you could do with some coffee. Joe, pour Mr Elliot a cup of coffee.'

Her attendant looked surly but picked up the coffee pot and promptly replaced it as Elliot shook his head.

'No, thank you, ma'am.'

His refusal surprised her and he saw a flicker of annoyance pass over her pretty features, but he knew that, although he had not eaten or drunk since early morning, he could not stop and make polite conversation with her – could not have spoken to anyone, in fact, except perhaps to talk about Jem, his danger, the necessity of doing something about it – fast! He began to turn his horse away, to ride off without another word, when a thought struck him.

'Listen, ma'am, I don't think you should be 'way out here, so far from home. There's dangerous men around ....'

'What men?' There was real irritation in her voice now, like a woman who feels she is being treated with indifference.

Elliot hesitated. Should he attempt to tell her about Jem, about Proctor, the half-breed, the Cheyenne, Jones, the gold ...? In his mind's eye, he saw her look of disbelief, her amusement, perhaps her contempt for the improbable yarn that he was coming out with.

'I've seen them.' He spoke as emphatically as he could in the hope of getting the warning through to her without further explanation. 'There's a gang of outlaws somewhere around and I think you would be a lot safer if you headed for home.'

'I am quite used to travel, thank you, Mr Elliot, and ...' – she laughed lightly in exaggerated amusement – 'I have Joe as my protector.'

Elliot looked at Joe. He was middle aged, dried-up looking, ill-tempered but maybe dependable. He looked as though he might be handy with that gun but it could be that he was turning a bit too old and too slow. Robert Campbell, the Indian Agent, must have confidence in him, however, since he was willing to leave his daughter in his care and Campbell was a smart man, fair with the Indians too, but maybe led around by the nose a bit by his pert and self-willed daughter.

'You see, Mr Elliot, I have my work to do among the Amerindians.'

The explanation was unnecessary, as they both knew, but was put forward in a deliberately superior and schoolmarmish voice which was intended to provoke him. Everyone in Red Creek knew about Miss Campbell and her Indian Studies, her college education back East and the book about the Plains Indians that she had been working on for God knows how long. Every summer, she spent time speaking and listening to the Indians on the reservation, and wandered around amongst them, taking notes, and camping out frequently, looked after by one or two more-or-less elderly retainers supplied by her anxious father. No Indian had ever shown her anything but respect, partly for her own sake and partly for the high regard in which the reservation Indians held her father, who was one of the few Indian Agents who tried to ensure them a measure of justice.

'Miss Campbell, they got my brother.' He told the story of Jem's disappearance quickly and briefly, not in expectation of getting help, but in the hope of driving home his warning. 'Now, I think you oughta head for some place safe. S'long, Miss Campbell!'

He rode off, unwilling to waste another moment, unaware of the expression of horror on her face, his mind full once again of Jem's situation, the meeting with the girl falling away behind him in his thoughts as he cantered along the trail which he hoped would lead to Proctor and his gang ....

Proctor knew by the signs that they were approaching the old mines. The trail they were now on, although long since fallen into disuse, looked as if it had been deliberately broadened out and smoothed well enough to take a mule cart. He had seen an old wheel rotting beside the track and other remnants of debris which told of past labour and activity. It was up this trail that the old-time miners had dragged their stores and their mining gear, with their hopes high and full of images of gold.

As he rode, Proctor too felt some of this excitement and elation. Somewhere up ahead, he was convinced, was a bag of gold that just awaited the finding, and on his journey across the valley, he had come around more and more firmly to the belief that it was hidden in the vicinity of Dead Mouth and that, with seven men searching methodically and looking for every trace of disturbance of the ground and poking into every nook and cranny, they would be pretty sure to find it. Billy Wolf had said also that Dead Mouth mine should be easy enough to recognize as he had heard that it got its name from the steep sided gulley in which it was situated.

In his mind's eye, Proctor saw himself putting his hands out to grasp that pile of gold and he realized that the only hands he wanted ever to be on it were his own ... but there was no way of ensuring that. It would have to be split seven ways and then he guessed that the gang would split up too and good riddance! Things had not been going well for a long time; nothing worthwhile had come their way for months and the men were restless and full of complaints and ready to blame him for their lack of success. So they would take their share of the gold and would spend it on drink and women and some of them would finish up pretty soon at the end of a rope as they were recognized in the townships for their past crimes. To Proctor it seemed like a complete waste of good money to let fools like Wilson and Pulley and Biss have a share – and as for that goddamned half-breed ....

But if they did not find the gold, what then? Proctor's mind turned cold at the thought. The gang would split up anyway but not peaceably. The men would be frustrated and angry and that could only mean recriminations and bloodshed.

'When the hell are we gonna see Chris? I gotta see Chris! I gotta speak to Chris!'

Jem's sudden outburst drew a flurry of curses down on his head and another blow into the small of his back. Over the past hours the boy had become more and more demented, constantly yelling out for his brother and crying and slobbering like a distressed child. The gang's patience with him had long since worn thin and their initial amused contempt had given way to irritation, ribald comment and insult. Time after time he had been cuffed around the head or punched in the ribs and his hands had been tied to the pommel of the saddle so that he could not scare the horse into bolting. His mount was now led by Haze who had amused himself on the journey by a constant stream of offensive remarks and jokes aimed at the unfortunate youth. To begin with Proctor had made some attempt to intervene, as he still had a lingering hope that the boy might remember something worthwhile, but sensing the mood of his men, and not wishing to strain his own waning influence by arguing about small matters, he had now withdrawn his protection, except to insist that he did not want the boy injured as he might still be useful with the Indians if they showed signs of making trouble.

Jem's cries and groans had now subsided as he lapsed into an almost trance-like state, and the party rode in silence for a time until interrupted by a shout from Lavelle, who was out in front.

'Injuns – up ahead!'

Proctor sat up, suddenly alert. They had seen small parties of Indians at various times all through the day but they had contented themselves by observing the group of white horsemen from a distance. Apart from telling his men to keep a sharp look-out in case of ambush, Proctor had taken no action. In this case, also, there did not seem to be any danger. The two redskins, young men mounted on ponies, turned away swiftly on realizing that they had been seen, and vanished from view.

'It beats me,' grumbled Pulley, 'why all this here land is laid out to be a reservation just for a pack o' stinkin' Injuns. Seems to me thet the US Army should just wipe them all out and be done with it and save everybody a whole deal o' trouble!'

'Yeah, you got it right,' growled Wilson. 'Goddamn gov'ment's goin' plumb crazy.'

'All this land. Oughta go to white folks,' continued Pulley. 'Plenty o' folks be mighty glad of it – seems to me.'

'My old Pa would'a been glad to get it,' remarked Biss, 'and he didn't have no time fer pesky Injuns either. Allus said "Only good Injun's a bad Injun".'

His recollections were drowned out by the loud guffaws of his companions.

'Your old Pappy got it wrong, Biss, the only good Injun's a dead Injun!'

'Well, thet's what I said.' Biss raised his voice in indignation. 'My old Pa fought the Shoshone an' the Sioux near all his life till he got a bullet in the knee that put him on crutches for the rest of it.'

'Yeah, I guess some o' them old-timers did a heap o' fightin' to clear the country o' them red varmints,' observed Haze.

'Killed three Injuns myself once,' smirked Wilson, with obvious pride. 'Just shot them down – one, two, three ....'

'Thet so,' drawled Billy, who had taken no part in the conversation up to this point, 'bet they was two old squaws and a bandy-legged kid.'

Wilson's mouth tightened but he remained silent, partly because Billy's remark was not too far from the truth but mainly because he knew that too many cracks against Indians could give rise to a dark mood in Billy Wolf which was best avoided.

The rest of the party sensed trouble and dropped the subject. The track was becoming steeper and was now leading through a clump of pine trees. All sat up in their saddles and looked around with some apprehension at the thought that this might be a place where they could perhaps be taken by surprise. However, they emerged from the dark tree cover without incident and saw, some distance ahead, a small, dilapidated looking cabin, partly overgrown by scrub set in a wide, clear space. Proctor raised his hand to bring the gang to a halt and examined it and the surrounding area as carefully as he could.

The place certainly looked deserted but he moved forward with considerable caution just the same, followed by the rest, all with hands ready on their guns. When they had approached within a few yards, Proctor dismounted, told his men to keep him covered, and pushed open the cabin door, which flapped wildly on its loose, leather hinges.

Inside was the smell of dust of years and the damp, musty odour of rotting wood. A broken iron stove lay on its side on the earth floor, two boxes stood near a corner beside a rusting shattered spade. A placard with the legend 'Home, Sweet Home' still decipherable, hung from the wall on a large hook of the kind usually employed to hang freshly killed game; an ancient scrap of newspaper moved uneasily in the draught. There was nothing else. No sign of recent disturbance, no sign that anyone had looked in here since the last miner had given up and moved on.

The sun was beginning to sink, sending a shaft of light through the tiny, open-shuttered window. Proctor realized that they had had a long hard day and it was about time they were making camp. The prospect of spending the night under a roof instead of in the open or under leaky canvas appealed to him.

'OK, boys, we've gone far enough. Let's call it a day.'

Outside, Lavelle had already dismounted and was standing, picking at his nose and looking about him, with an air of casual curiosity, at the scraps of sackcloth, metal and wood which lay all around, mostly half-buried in the earth and stones.

'Don't look to me, boss, as if this be a mine. Don't look like to 've been no gold-diggin' round hereabouts.'

Proctor nodded slow agreement. This place was an outlying shack, a shelter for men driving muleteams up to the mines, a convenient spot to split up a long journey. The mines must be still a considerable way up ahead. Nevertheless, he felt excited at the realization that they were at last approaching their goal. The impulse to push on was still with him, competing with the need to make camp. His eyes followed the track which was still discernible as it led further up the ragged hillside before vanishing around an overhanging rockface.

'Listen, I want to have a look-see a bit up that trail. Still some daylight left, so we may as well scout up ahead aways. Haze – you, Wilson an' Pulley stay here and get a fire started. We could all do with some hot food and coffee. Gonna sleep real warm an' comfortable tonight!' He rubbed his hands together in exaggerated enthusiasm, almost as if he expected their admiration for his sagacity and good humour.

Haze looked doubtful.

'Think it's a good idea to split up? What about them Injuns?'

To Proctor, it was beginning to look as if the possible danger of attack had been blown up out of proportion. These reservation Indians were not looking for trouble though there was always the chance ....

'Keep a good look-out and fire off a couple of shots if you see any sign o' them gophers. We ain't goin' far anyhow.' He looked around at the wide space surrounding the shack. 'You kin keep 'em off here easy enough if they start anythin' but I don't reckon they will.'

Haze, Wilson and Pulley watched Proctor and his companions as they gradually disappeared from view. They were glad enough to dismount to ease their aching limbs but the prospect of making an immediate start on the chores of firelighting and cooking, simple enough though they were, seemed too irksome at that moment. Wilson glowered and spat on the ground.

'Big gas-bag! Always gotta be shootin' his mouth off. Why don't he make the goddam coffee?' He kicked savagely at a piece of broken planking. 'What the hell does he know about Injuns?'

'Well, may as well make a start.' Pulley picked up some fragments of wood in a listless manner.

Wilson stood with his thumbs in his belt and scowled into the evening sky. Apart from his saddle-sore weariness, he was plagued by an almost overwhelming sense of disappointment. When they had come across the old miners' trail he had felt sure that they were just about at the end of this journey and could set into the task of finding the gold without further delay. Now he saw that they had a long way to go yet and, not only that, but the suspicion that Proctor's confidence in finding the stuff was misplaced was beginning to surface in his mind to an extent that it had not done before.

He was aware of Pulley wandering about, picking up

more scraps of firewood and he turned his eyes towards him, thinking that he had better show willing and make a start too, when he found himself looking at Jem who, finding himself disregarded, had sat down on the ground and was staring into space as he drifted into a world of his own.

Wilson's eyes narrowed. He strode over to the boy and kicked him in the back.

'Hey, you, ya lazy skunk, git up on yer feet an' git ta work! Git some o' thet wood broke up right now! Ya know what wood is, don't ya? Wood – W.O.O.D – wood! Git movin'!'

Jem grunted with pain and, startled out of his daydream, rubbed his back. His eyes opened wide, staring at Wilson, as if seeing him for the first time.

'Hey, you shouldn't a' done thet! I'm gonna tell Chris ya done thet!'

'Chris! Goddam Chris! Thet's 'bout all ya kin say, ya dumb eedjit! Chris! Chris! Chris!'

Jem stared harder at Wilson's leering face as realization dawned.

'You're the feller thet Chris punched right off the sidewalk! You was rollin' about in the dirt ...!'

The hot anger of Wilson's eyes chilled. He stood still, scarcely breathing, then his voice came, hard – metallic.

'You got some helluva memory when it suits ya, boy.' He reached out and took Jem by the collar. 'Think ya kin make a fool outa me, do ya?' He hauled Jem to his feet and swung him around. He struck out, bringing a spot of blood to the youth's lip. 'Think ya kin make fools out of all of us?' He punched Jem violently in the chest so that he staggered backwards towards the door of the shack. 'You know somethin' about thet gold, an' you'd better start talkin'. I ain't as dumb as goddamn Proctor!' He struck hard – again and again.

'Hey,' Pulley sounded anxious, scared. 'Go easy. The boss said he wasn't ta be knocked 'round too much!'

'Thet's been the trouble all along – Proctor

nursemaidin' this lunkhead! We shoulda had thet gold an' been outa here long since!'

He struck out again. Jem's face was red and bleeding. His eyes streamed childish tears. His arms waved wildly, one hand groping for a grip on the doorpost. Another blow sent him sprawling through and on to the earthen floor. Wilson stepped in after him, fists still raised.

Pulley looked at Haze as if for guidance and shrugged his shoulders. Haze smiled thinly with faint amusement, then they followed Wilson into the darkening interior of the shack.

FOUR

A breeze moved faintly in the height of the pines, breaking the late afternoon sunlight into dappled, shifting patterns. These high tops and tender branches made, under its influence, a rustle and a sigh, only audible because of the intense silence all around. The air was heavy with the scent of pine resin and the carpet of pine needles seemed designed to deaden all sound in the cathedral-like stillness. From time to time, some small bird fluttered its brilliance from shade to light and then once more to shade, as if aware that its small presence was enough to disturb the age-long contemplation of the trees.

Elliot had sat for a long time in this semi-darkness, his body taut in the saddle, his eyes peering through the avenue of dark trunks to the wide sunlit space beyond. The tiny almost derelict shack caught the full glare of the sun and cast its own deep shadow on to the disturbed earth around it.

He knew that they had been there. The trail that they had followed led to it and he could make out some trace of the same track snaking further amid the overhanging rock. There was no sign of life anywhere now, though; no men, no horses nor any movement or sound. Still, he waited, anxious to be certain that he was placing himself at no disadvantage.

He was sure that, up to now, they could not be certain that he was on their trail. He had come across their tracks the day before on the old gold trail and believed himself to be perhaps half a day or more behind them but he had followed on with caution, keen – if at all possible – to keep the element of surprise. Deliberately, he had avoided sticking too close to the tracks, but had ridden off to one side, taking advantage of every scrap of cover that the country held, and for the last half-mile, had ridden through the trees, keeping parallel to the old mining road without showing himself upon it ....

He knew, just the same, that he would have to venture into the open. There was no easy way of skirting around this place and he felt, in any case, that he must take a closer look. Judging by the churned up soil in the vicinity of the shack, they had spent some time there, maybe even camped for the night, and he might find out something more about them. Although he knew from the tracks that there was quite a bunch of them – maybe five or six – he had not been able to discern the exact number but perhaps by careful examination of the ground in the camp he could form a better idea.

Although there were various hiding places amongst the rocks further up the slopes from which a man with a rifle could command the entire area, he was gradually becoming convinced that there was no such danger and that the gang had moved on, in all probability still unaware of his approach. Slowly, he urged his mount forward, ducking his head slightly here and there to avoid low branches, but never taking his eyes off the shack and its surroundings.

As he came towards the edge of the wood, he caught the strong smell of the ashes of a burnt-out camp-fire and saw the blackened spot where it had been. He knew by the heaviness of its scent that it was hours old and the horse dung lying around had been dried out by the long sunlight of the day. Nevertheless, he advanced with undiminished caution, his gaze fixed upon the door and the tiny window of the shack but with the outer borders of his sight alert to any movement amid the cover of the slopes and his ears straining for the slightest sound.

As he approached, he observed that the door of the shack had been torn from its hinges and lay half blocking the entrance. The shutters of the small window were ajar and he could almost see into the dim interior. There was just blankness there ... blankness and something vaguely pale. His finger crept towards the trigger. Something pale ... a faint blur ... no trace of movement but a faint blur ... a pale blur beginning to resolve itself into a ... a face! He spurred his horse forward and around the corner of the shack. Without drawing rein, he leapt from the saddle, rifle in hand. As his feet touched the earth, he struck his mount on the hindquarters so that it trotted onwards for a short distance so that whoever was in the shack could not be certain that he had dismounted.

He remained quite still, listening intently for the first sign of movement, half expecting the man lying in wait to step outside in the hope of putting a bullet into his back as he rode towards cover. But there was no sound – only his own subdued breathing and the beating of his heart.

At this end of the building, there were no windows so there was no chance of leaping up to put in a hasty shot, but, on the other hand, he felt confident that he could not be surprised as there was no way that anyone could get out through the door and make his way to the corner without some sound – however faint.

He waited for a long time. Whoever was inside was content to lie low until he made the next move. Possibly the man did not realize that he had been seen and still expected to lie in ambush, to wait until Elliot had finished looking around outside, had dropped his guard, and then to blast him as he came through the door, convinced that no one was within.

But this situation could not go on. The outlaw in the shack had obviously been expecting him and, that being the case, the rest must be somewhere in the neighbourhood, ready to give support, possibly to shoot Elliot down from somewhere overhead.

He took his eyes from the corner for a moment and

looked up to the rocky hillside. There was no doubt that
he was a sitting duck in his present position, although he
still could not see any sign of danger from that direction.
It could only be that, for some reason, their plans had
gone wrong; their attention had been drawn elsewhere
and they had not yet seen him, although they soon
would. Maybe the man inside had guessed that and was
waiting to hear them start shooting before he joined in
the fray.

So there was no time to be lost. If he could finish off
this guy, he could prepare himself for attack from the
others. He crept as quietly as possible around the shack
on the opposite side from the window until he turned
the corner near to the door. There was no more time for
hesitation. He drew a deep breath. Now was the time to
move. Now he must advance into the attack! He leapt
across the threshold, crouching as he went, bringing his
rifle up to aim in one swift movement, pointing the
barrel at the figure by the wall, aiming at the chest,
finger beginning to tighten on the trigger, preparing to
squeeze, to pump out the bullet, to blast into the flesh
and bone of ... of ... of Jem! For Christ sake! Of Jem!
Jem hanging there by the wall, body contorted, face ...
Oh, God, the face ...! Twisted and blackened, eyes wide
and dead, tongue thrusting between swollen lips!

Elliot dropped to his knees, his rifle falling from his
hands. His eyes were wide and staring, seeming to
unwittingly mock the wild, empty eyes of the hanging
corpse before him. His mind refused to take in what he
was seeing. His brother – his kid brother – dead,
tortured, garrotted. My God! He covered his face with
his hands as if to blot out some crazy hallucination. He
crouched there like a beaten animal, afraid to look up,
afraid to move, afraid to face the nightmare reality ....

He came up slowly, as a drowning man who cannot
help but to prolong his despair. The arms that thrust him
upwards from the earthen floor trembled in their task.
At length he was on his feet, bending forward slightly as

if unsure of his balance. The hanging form before him filled up his mind, blotting out the rest of the world. He had seen corpses before – by the score, by the hundreds – he had seen hanged men, but this bore no relation to any of these past events. This seemed a crime beyond the senseless cruelty of man: it seemed to him to be the foul deed of some loathsome fiend and the sight of it drove a leaden blade deep within him.

By degrees, he took control of himself. The tide of shuddering that had swept through his body ebbed a little and he forced himself to step forward, his fingers fumbling for the knife at his belt. In a moment, he had cut through the rope which suspended Jem's body from the hook in the wall and lowered him gently to the floor. He cut through the thongs around the swollen wrists and then groped, with a resurgence of shuddering, for the noose buried in the flesh of the neck. Jem's face floated before him, twisted, tortured and ugly in its death throes. Blood and saliva had congealed over the mouth and chin. There were cuts and bruises only partly concealed in the blackened, purple hues of his skin.

Elliot stretched out the body of his brother upon the floor as straight as it would lie and then went outside to his saddle-bag and brought in his cape to spread over the head and shoulders. He then went back outside and stood, one hand on the frame of the doorway, and tried to think with some degree of calm. For some moments, he could not do so. His mind seemed stunned – blank. He looked, without seeing, at the sun-baked rocks and the swaying pines and into the depths of the sky, where a hawk hovered and swooped. For moments he felt crushed and defeated, then the leaden blade in his heart began to burn and the blaze of anger and hatred spread through him, so that he had to fight against the impulse to mount up at once and to set off in haste to destroy the men who had done the innocent foolishness of Jem to death like the murder of a child.

These men were, he knew, drawing ever further away. They would spend some time searching for the gold which had attracted them here to this region, but there was no way of guessing how long they would take in their search or how many days would pass before they rode far out of his reach. Nevertheless, something had to be done about Jem. He could not be left where he was to be gnawed at by coyotes or torn by wolves. The homestead was a long way back now, as was Red Creek, and to carry the body back there for burial and then return was tantamount to giving up the chase. There was nothing for it but to try to bury Jem here. It might only take an hour or so and then he could get on the trail once more.

He searched around and found a broken spade on the floor of the hut. What remained of the handle was short and splintered but he used it to hack and hew, regardless of his bleeding hands. The ground was full of small stones and boulders. The work was painfully slow and soon he began to sweat and pant with his efforts and to feel a sense of rising desperation as he realized how long the task was likely to take.

He was bending forward to lever out a large chunk of rock when he heard a slight sound and he spun round to pick up his rifle from the side of the grave but his hand touched nothing but pebbles and gritty earth ....

There was a young Indian standing a few paces from the graveside. In his hands he held a lance of the type used by the Plains Indians in their buffalo hunts. Its fire-hardened point was turned, not towards Elliot, but slightly to one side, as if in defence. A yard or two further back crouched another redskin of about the same age, holding Elliot's rifle. Their eyes, although wary, were not hostile but when he made to move towards them, lance point and rifle turned to threaten him.

Something in their demeanour told him that they did not intend mere theft and he remained still awaiting

their next move. As he looked over the shoulder of the
youth with the rifle and out past the corner of the shack,
he saw a small cavalcade of Indians emerging slowly
from the pine woods. There were perhaps about a
dozen, mostly young braves, but seemingly led by the
two grey-haired old chiefs in the front of the group.
Two or three squaws and a boy leading two spare ponies
took up the rear.

Within minutes, they had formed a ragged semi-circle
around him, as if to prevent him reaching his horse,
which stood patiently by the hut. One of the old men
urged his mount forward a few paces as if to establish
his authority. He had the wizened, leathery look of a
man who has spent a lifetime in the sun and wind and
the snows of the plains. From his straggly hair hung a
bedraggled arrangement of black feathers centred upon
a tiny circle of raven skin. An ancient shield of buffalo
hide upon which the tribal totem of the raven, painted
black on red, could still be discerned in spite of years of
weathering, hung at his side. His pony looked tired and
emaciated. A ragged poultice of leaves, bound with
birch bark, did little to cover up a festering sore on its
foreleg.

After another prolonged silence, the old man spoke in
the jerking faintly sing-song language of his race. The
youth with the lance listened with care and then
translated to Elliot. His English was halting but clear,
like that of an intelligent, quick-to-learn youngster who
has lived in the proximity of white people.

'Grey Lynx say that this land all belong Absarokee. It
has been given to us by the white chief, Campbell. You
must go away. Go back to Red Creek.'

Elliot shook his head. 'Tell your chief that I respect his
right to the land but a great crime has been committed
against me and I must follow the men who have done it.
I'm talking about the men who were here. These men.'
He pointed at the hoofmarks and prints all around.
'Have you not seen these men?'

The young man repeated his words in Absarokee and again came back with an answer.

'Grey Lynx and the Absarokee know about these white men who have come uninvited to our territory. We do not like these men but you must still return to Red Creek. You should not be here. The chief, Campbell, promised this.'

Elliot understood. The Absarokee, like other redskins who eventually found themselves on the reservations had learned the hard way that fighting against the whites could lead only to disaster. They were afraid to oppose Proctor and his gang, not only because the group of whites formed a formidable enough force, but because white opinion in general would not have it that Indians should fight against whites of any description, even a bunch of renegades. If any white justice was to be handed out, it must only come from the whites themselves. The old chief knew that the little security his tribe enjoyed depended upon keeping the favour of the white government. There was too much at stake to risk a serious tangle with Proctor's men. Exerting a little forceful persuasion on a lone white, like himself, might, on the other hand, be possible.

Elliot did not resent their attitude but he had no intentions of giving way to it. He spoke slowly and with emphasis.

'These men have murdered my brother. I am goin' to find them and I am goin' to give them what they deserve. Nothin' is goin' to stop me from gettin' to them as long as I can move. I have no quarrel with the Absarokee but you must not try to prevent me from doin' what is right.'

This time the young man did not translate immediately. He had seen Elliot looking past him at the shack as he spoke, the troubled expression and had detected the grief in his voice. His eyes reflected surprise, apprehension and sympathy in rapid succession.

'You are the brother of Crazy Man?' He jerked his head slightly towards the shack. 'Crazy Man is in the house. Crazy Man is dead.'

Elliot stared at him.

'How do you know that?'

The youth waved his hand towards the young brave with the rifle.

'He, Star Song, come here in morning. See Crazy Man dead.' He spoke at some length to the old chief, who consulted with the other old man before making his reply. 'Grey Lynx say bad medicine Crazy Man dead. Bad medicine to stop your revenge. You must go on your war-path.' He looked at the half-dug hole in which Elliot still stood. 'Grey Lynx say Absarokee carry away Crazy Man.'

Elliot looked at him doubtfully. An Indian funeral for Jem with his corpse left to rot on a raised platform did not seem to be acceptable in spite of the poor alternative. However, before he could reply, the youth seemed to divine his thoughts and spoke again.

'We take Crazy Man to Campbell. Have Christian burial.'

Elliot suddenly felt profoundly relieved. Campbell would know what to do and if he, Elliot, ever got back, he would settle matters in any way that seemed appropriate.

They went into the shack, placed a large Indian blanket on the floor, and lifted Jem on to it. They wrapped up the body and tied it round with cords before carrying it outside and laying it across the back of a pony. As the corpse was carried out, the women began to wail and chant. Elliot fought to curb the trembling sensation which threatened to return. With a slight gesture of farewell, the old chief turned away, followed by his people. For a brief moment, only the two young men remained behind. Star Song handed Elliot back his rifle with grave courtesy and then mounted up. The youth with the lance dallied for a moment longer as if he

felt there was something more to be said, some question
which remained unanswered. Elliot knew what the
question was but asked another one instead.

'How many white men were here?' He waved his hand
at the tracks which surrounded them.

The Absarokee held up eight fingers and then
lowered one hastily. So they had counted Jem as part of
the gang. Elliot felt absurdly hurt by the natural error
but nodded his head in understanding.

'Seven white men?' He felt somehow that it was
important to get the number right. Very soon he would
be up against them. He had to know.

The youth shook his head, held up six fingers and
then made the sign for the half-breed by drawing a
finger down through the centre of his face.

So there were seven in the gang. The odds were grim.
The worst he had ever known but he knew that that in
itself could make no difference to his course of action.
Whether there were seven or seventy, he had to go
against them. It was madness but a worse form of
madness would be to do nothing; to go back to the
homestead and to sit at the stove and to see Jem's face
and to hear Jem's voice all around; to hear him ask, time
after time, in his persistent way, why he had done
nothing, why Chris had let them get away with it, why
they had gone free after the torture and murder they
had committed .... That way would lead to madness. He
felt that to be certain. The other certainty was death. It
was possible, with the advantage of surprise, that he
might kill two of them. He might take out Proctor, who
had instigated the whole thing, and the half-breed, who
had taken Jem from his home but he, himself, would be
number three. He could not kill them all though he
knew them all to be guilty. He knew that it was a battle
that he could not survive but he found himself facing
that prospect without fear of any other emotion except
the hatred and desire for revenge which raged within.

He became aware that the young Indian was still

speaking. The youth's tone was earnest, almost appealing.

'The Absarokee are not afraid. We have always been warriors. But we cannot fight the White Man. Bad medicine to fight White Man ....'

'I know you are not afraid.' For all his own turmoil of thought, Elliot felt sympathy for the young man who was so anxious not to be regarded as a coward. 'I know why ya can't do nothin' about these white men. I understand. They're bad medicine – I know that!'

They were too. Proctor and his gang were bad medicine all right. Bad medicine for Jem, for himself, for everybody. He walked over to the shack and picked up his cape which lay at the door and put it into his saddle-bag. He then mounted the dappled horse, his face set and troubled, and turned on to the trail which led around the hanging rocks. His mind was already laden with the task before him and he did not look back at the young Absarokee who stood still, lance in hand, and watched him depart.

FIVE

To his surprise, Elliot found the remains of the gang's night camp within two miles of the shack. It was on a grassy slope where the marks of bivouac tents were still visible and an area had been cropped short by tethered horses. There were the blackened ashes of a camp-fire with traces of spilled coffee and masses of footprints all around.

He followed the tracks of the morning leading from it and as dusk began to fall, forced himself to halt. For the second night in succession he camped without a fire and ate dried meat and biscuit and drank stale water from his canteen. He wrapped in his blanket and lay, looking into the night sky and burning with his anger and bitterness. For hour after hour, sleep eluded him and when it came, in fits and starts, his dreams were filled with images of Jem's face, ugly in its pain and fear ....

He arose at the first grey light of dawn, glad to stand up to ease his cold, stiff body, and to lose no more time in picking up their trail once again. It was easy enough to follow, with so many horses and no attempt at concealment. Mostly, they kept to the beaten track of the old mining days but, as the day wore on, he became aware of riders having moved off to one side or the other before returning, of stoppages as if for discussion or argument, of a general feeling of indiscipline and lack of cohesion. By the late afternoon, he was passing through a region where the old trail linked up with rugged canyons which led off into the steep hills àll around. These had no established trails through them but he saw evidence of one or two riders having turned off into these, as if to explore them, before rejoining the old road and catching up with their companions.

By late afternoon, he felt that he was beginning to close the gap between himself and the gang but resisted the temptation to hurry on. Instead he advanced with increased caution, looking all the time for some easily accessible point of vantage from which he might be able to view the country ahead. At last, he reached a place where the trail led across a narrow valley and could be seen wending its way over the saddleback ridge between two hills ahead. The area was more open than much of the country he had been travelling through and consisted of rolling slopes of grass and brush dotted with outcrops of stone. The hill to the right presented a slope which seemed not too difficult, and he turned off on to it and gradually made the ascent, choosing a route which would not overstrain his horse but would take him as close as possible to the summit before he was forced to dismount.

The top of the hill was mostly bare rock and he climbed towards it with great caution, determined not to show himself against the skyline. At length, he reached a point from which he could observe the country ahead, and lay beside a boulder, straining his eyes against the red light of the setting sun and the contrasting dark shadows cast by the ridges and huge outcrops of rock of the rugged landscape which reared up once more into the distance. From where he lay, the old mining trail could no longer be seen but he could make a guess at its general direction and, as he peered through the confusing mixture of light and dark, he saw what he had hoped would be there – a far off glint of a camp-fire.

The sight of it sent the adrenalin flowing through his veins. That was where Proctor and his gang of murderers were at this precise moment! A few miles more and he could be upon them. The desire to ride pell-mell up the trail and to go in shooting was almost overwhelming but he knew that would achieve nothing. He would be detected and shot down before he could get to grips with them. All the element of surprise would be lost, which was all he had in his favour. What he would do, however, would be to advance as close as was safe to their camp that evening and then, in the early dawn, before the faintest glimmer of morning light, he would go into the camp on foot, find and kill Proctor and then the half-breed and then keep shooting until he was downed. He would, almost certainly, be the third to die but at least Jem would be partly avenged.

The plan, crude though it was, gave him some slight peace of mind. He remained still for some time, savouring the thought of the bullets smashing into these evil men, his own death seeming almost a trivial matter after such satisfaction.

When he returned to his horse, he led her gently and slowly down the slope along the edge of the hillside until the footing was good enough for riding. The light was beginning to fade but he could still make out some features of rocky outcrop which he had noted lay near to the old trail and he made his way towards them by degrees, feeling that he had time enough to get close to his objective before darkness fell altogether but that to hurry along the trail in the light that remained could put his plan in jeopardy.

He still had some distance to go before meeting up with the track when he drew in the reins abruptly, his body tense, his breath suddenly stilled. He had seen a movement on the trail ahead … a shadow which had passed behind the deeper shadow of high rock. He waited, one hand touching the butt of his rifle, and saw a figure appear, more quickly than he had expected, from the other end of the long rock shadow. It was a man on horseback, leaning forward slightly in the saddle and looking ahead, with some air of tension, up the trail as it wound its way over the narrow pass between the twin hills.

There was something vaguely familiar about the posture of the rider but in that light and at that distance he could not be sure. He had little time to think about it, in any case, as a second figure appeared immediately following behind the first. This time there was no room for doubt. She sat up straight in the saddle, dark hair only partly covered by her broad-brimmed hat, red jacket catching the red of the sunset ....

Elliot grunted in amazement and then groaned inwardly. Here they were, Joe, Miss Campbell and the pack horse, plodding up that dangerous trail almost as if she were on the way home from Church! The fool of a woman! Did she not know of the danger up ahead? Had she not listened to his warning? Obviously she had not and had little idea of what she could be getting into.

Elliot's first impulse was to call out but he restrained himself as the habit of caution which had been with him for days brought its influence to bear. Proctor's camp was still some miles ahead and he believed he had time to catch up on her. To call out might put them in greater danger as sound could echo and re-echo through the cliffs and gullies that lay all around. He spurred his horse forward as they moved up the track which crossed the low saddleback of hill and disappeared. Still, he felt confident that he could overtake them and when he did so, he would make certain this time that his warning got through – and if she would not listen, he would make sure that Joe did, and between them, they would force her to turn back and get down the valley and out of danger.

Cursing under his breath, he trotted across the rough grass and scrub towards the old trail but had gone only a short distance when a shot rang out. He reined in again, uncertain for a moment of its direction. Then he heard two more in rapid succession and he realized that they had come from somewhere around the narrow pass over which the party had just gone. Seconds later, a rider appeared around the corner of the trail – a rider who swayed wildly in the saddle, while his panic-stricken mount left the track and raced madly in the general direction of Elliot. As the animal bounded across the rough ground, its rider suddenly dropped, and was dragged, with one foot jammed in a stirrup, for some yards before his foot was torn free and his mount, relieved of its burden, galloped with increased speed off into the shadows of the darkening valley.

Elliot spurred forward, almost heedless of the uncertain ground, pulling his rifle from its place by the saddle as he went. Another rider, this time the girl, hurtled down the trail, holding grimly on as her horse plunged and slithered on the shifting scree and loose dirt. It too left the trail and galloped off on the other side, away from Elliot, and he saw then, to his intense dismay, that she was hotly pursued by two others, low in the saddle, guns waving in hands, yelling and hooting as they gained upon her.

Her horse had travelled no great distance when it came to an abrupt, bone-breaking halt as a hoof went into a hole in the ground or became stuck between boulders. It lunged forward and the girl was thrown violently over its neck. She struck the ground, rolled over once, and lay still. The two men, almost upon her, drew up, leapt from the saddle and ran towards her prone form, waving their arms and capering in obvious delight.

Anger drove through Elliot, crackling and blazing like a brush fire. To see, at last, these murderers who had tortured and killed his kid brother was maddening enough and to see them still killing and delighting in their viciousness was beyond endurance. He urged his mount to a gallop, passing the corpse of Joe, who lay upon his back, chest a gory mass of red, eyes staring blindly into the darkening sky, and was across the old trail and riding down upon them within moments. He gave no thought to the notion of coming to a halt and attempting to shoot them down from a distance. The need to get to grips with them was too strong and blotted out any other course of action. As he rode, he swung out his rifle, gripping it tightly at the trigger guard, stock held firmly against the inside of his forearm. His face was set in rage, his mind intent on its one purpose.

The two outlaws, absorbed for the moment in their victory, did not become aware of his approach until the thundering of hooves gave them only seconds of warning. Pulley let go of the girl's skirts and straightened up, half turning his head as he did so. The heavy rifle barrel, swung with the impetus of the horse and rider behind it, struck him across the temple with bone-splitting force and he toppled like a pole-axed steer to the ground.

In the next instant, Elliot – suddenly fearful that the flaying hooves would trample upon the still form of the girl – tugged violently at the reins, pulling his mount's head around and bringing it to a wild, stumbling halt. From the corner of his eye, he could see the other man, tousled red hair stringing across his forehead, scampering backwards, hand already going for the gun at his hip. He pulled the dappled horse around as far as it would go in order to ride down the man but the animal was confused and afraid and reared and stamped in terror. Elliot put his spurs to it to drive it in the new direction but the outlaw's gun was out of its holster and two shots rang out, ill-aimed, panicky shots but Elliot felt the dappled horse shudder as the bullets ploughed into her ....

As the horse slumped to the ground, Elliot leapt clear to avoid being trapped beneath her weight, slid down behind the cover of her body and brought his rifle round to the firing position almost in one swift movement. The red-haired man squeezed the trigger once again but this time there was no sound but the click of an empty gun. He turned and ran towards his horse, which had moved away nervously from the mêlée, and was pulling himself into the saddle when Elliot's bullet struck into his back. For a second, it seemed that he would topple over the other side of his mount, but he held on desperately to the pommel and then leaned forward over the horse's neck as it cantered off through the scrub.

Elliot aimed once more, confident that he would bring the man crashing down, but, in a sudden paroxysm of pain, the wounded animal beneath him made a wild, heaving movement which knocked up the barrel of the rifle and sent the shot wide of the mark.

For a brief moment, Elliot lay still, gathering his breath, then he pulled himself upright and moved over towards the girl. As he did so, he almost trod upon the grinning dead face of the man he had felled and paused for a fleeting moment as he recognized him as one of the men who had been with Proctor that day at the farm gate.

The sense of grim satisfaction left him at once as he leaned over the girl. She lay on her back, eyes closed, face pale in the dimming light. One arm was twisted grotesquely beneath her but she made no movement or sound. He dropped to his knees beside her and was relieved to realize that she was still breathing. He put a hand under her head and felt the stickiness of blood in the softness of her hair. Hastily, he went back to his saddle-bag for his canteen of water and felt a tinge of real regret that the dappled horse was dead.

The girl did not respond as he bathed her face in the tepid water and he began to feel an anxiety greater than any he had felt since the death of his brother. When he straightened out her arm from beneath her body, he saw that it was badly broken. He stood up then and looked around, uncertain of his next move. It was obvious that even if the rest of the gang were camped beside the fire he had seen in the distance, they would have heard the shots and would be on their way to investigate. Quite possibly some of them were nearer than that and there was no way that he could defend himself in this place. He would be immediately surrounded and shot down and it did not require much imagination to realize what would happen to the girl.

The horse that had belonged to the outlaw at his feet stood still a short distance away. It was a sorry-looking creature but all that he had. His own horse was dead, the girl's horse lay, broken-legged and agonized. Pity for the animal's suffering swept through him and he took the revolver from the corpse and was about to use it when he realized that another shot would only bring Proctor and his men the more certainly upon him. Reluctantly, he killed the animal with his knife, opening up the heavy veins of the neck so that it bled quickly to death.

He had turned back to the girl and was trying to discover the extent of her head injury when he heard the sound of a horse approaching slowly through the grass and scrub. He swung round, rifle up and pointing, believing that this was the end now ... this must be his final few moments ... this was when he had to die. However, even in the twilight, he could see at once that there was only one rider coming towards him.

The horseman was partially silhouetted against the greying pink of the skyline and, as he drew nearer, it became clear that he was a redskin. The feathers in his hair bobbed with the jogging movement of his mount and he held up one hand in a sign that he came in peace. When he had approached within a few yards, he stopped and looked at Elliot for a long moment, as if attempting to read his thoughts.

Even if Elliot had not known almost at once who the man was, he would have known that this was no reservation Indian. This man belonged to one of the still untamed tribes and was dressed for war. His brow was darkened by the black stripes which spoke of his willingness to accept death; the lower half of his face, from the bridge of the nose to the chin, was covered by the yellow ochre of the Earth, his mother, who would sustain him in battle. From his neck hung a necklace of bear claws and his buckskin shirt was decorated with omens of war. From the shoulder of his skewbald pony there hung a long-barrelled gun of an antiquated type of the sort often carried by Indians, more for prestige than for use, since they could seldom obtain enough ammunition to become skilled in handling them. At his back, however, he carried a more practical weapon in the form of a bow and a quiver full of arrows – these fletched, in the Cheyenne fashion, by the striped feathers of the wild turkey.

'You are brother of Crazy Man.' He was soft spoken but had the air of a mature man of about thirty years old. 'Crazy Man dead.'

Elliot fought down the irritation which he felt at the name given to Jem, as he knew that no disrespect was intended. In fact, as he was well aware, the reverse was true.

'Yes,' he replied, simply. 'He is dead.'

'Crazy Man killed by bad men. Jones killed by bad men. Jones friend to Cheyenne. Crazy Man friend to all Indian.' He leaned down from his pony's back as if to confide. 'Half Yellow Face take war-path. You take war-path. We are brothers? We go kill bad men?'

Elliot, for the first time in many days, felt his spirits rise. The prospect of having an ally in his fight against Proctor filled him with a sense of relief which went beyond the practical help which this one Indian could be expected to give him.

'Yeah, we both have good reason for killing these men.'

The Cheyenne slipped from his pony and looked at the dead outlaw. 'You have counted coup. Good warrior.' His voice held genuine admiration but then he pointed towards the nearby hill. 'Men come soon.'

He turned then and looked straight at the still figure

of the girl, showing no surprise, as if he had known all along of her presence but had chosen to ignore her.

'Woman not dead. Woman hurt.'

Elliot recognized the question that lay behind these simple statements. What was Elliot going to do about the woman? In the mind of the Cheyenne the woman presented no problem since few Indians would turn aside from a chosen war-path for the sake of a woman, whatever her predicament, but the mind of a white man was different and Elliot realized that this Indian understood that as a fact though probably not the reasoning behind it.

For the first time, Elliot became suddenly fully aware of his dilemma. He could not leave Julie Campbell where she was. That had always been out of the question. He must do all he could to save her and that could only mean taking her back to a place of safety. Whether he could, in fact, accomplish that might be doubtful, but it was certain that he must do everything in his power to help her.

And, yet, if he succeeded in doing that, how could he ever settle with Proctor? Success in rescuing the girl must mean failure to destroy the scum who had murdered Jem! Jem's death would go unavenged and how could he, Elliot, who had sworn in his own mind, maybe in the presence of the soul of his kid brother, to take this revenge, ever live with himself afterwards? How could he let Proctor and his gang ride off, with or without that gold, still chuckling at what they had done to the boy?

He stood, overcome with dismay, for a long moment, and then looked into the glittering dark eyes of the Cheyenne.

'I must help the woman. That must be done.'

The Indian remounted and turned away. After a few yards, he stopped and looked back.

'This place bad medicine. You die if men come. You go soon.'

He rode off into the gathering darkness while Elliot bent once again over Julie Campbell.

SIX

The high roof of the sky changed slowly to a maze of stars as Elliot attended to the girl, binding up her head wound as best he could and feeling in the dim light for the two breaks in her arm in a rough attempt to set them, before tying it in a crude splint made of tough scrub branches, cut with great difficulty, from the vegetation all around.

As he worked, he became more and more aware of the desperate plight they were in. The girl showed no signs of regaining consciousness and was obviously unfit to ride out of this dangerous place. Even with Elliot leading the outlaw's horse, she would not be able to sit in the saddle and he had seen, more than once, the deaths of men with head wounds, who had been slung roughly across the backs of their mounts in a vain attempt to rescue them from similar situations.

So there was nothing for it except to wait here until she was fit to ride but, with the crude medical attention he was able to give her and their lack of water and food, there seemed little prospect that that would ever happen. It was much more likely that she would weaken and die even if they were not discovered and killed.

As he cut the rough twigs and ripped up the dead man's shirt to bind the splint, he kept a sharp look-out, expecting the arrival of his enemies at any moment.

To his surprise, time went by with no sign of their approach but he knew that he could not afford to relax his vigilance and resolved to remain awake and to be

ready for them. The girl was now lying quietly and
seemed to be breathing in a more normal manner and
he covered her with his blanket as the chill of the night
descended. For hours he sat, watching the pass and the
surrounding heights, attempting to retain his concentra-
tion in spite of the troubled thoughts which crowded
into his mind. At some point, weariness got the better of
him, and he dozed off, only to awaken with a start at the
sound of a gunshot which may have been real and far
off or possibly just some figment of his dreams. He sat,
tense and alert, waiting for it to be repeated but the
night remained silent ....

He was awakened again, in the greyness of early
dawn, by the fluttering of ravens as they picked over the
carcasses. They flew off as he stood up, rifle already in
hands, annoyed with himself for sleeping. There was a
mist hanging all around, clothing the slopes and heights
and creating strange shapes from the rocks. There was
no sign of danger but he saw that they had been joined
by another horse, the pack animal which he had last
seen following in the rear of the little cavalcade as it
disappeared over the pass. The beast stood next to the
outlaw's horse, which he had tethered some short
distance away on the previous evening when it showed
signs of being nervous and restless in the proximity of
the dead animals, and now both seemed to wait, content
with each other's company.

He made the pack animal fast and then came back
quickly, anxious to see how the girl now was. She
opened her eyes as he bent over her and looked
surprised and puzzled to see him. She attempted to
speak but no sound came to her lips and her effort to
raise herself upwards a little failed and she sank back as
if exhausted. Elliot motioned for her to remain still, and
then went back to the pack horse. It was well laden with
tents, cooking gear and canvas bags that he guessed
contained food and water. As his hands explored the
animal's load, he felt hope rising as he realized that if

they were forced to remain here for some days, and were not attacked, he could now provide some shelter for the girl and better food than he had carried with him.

Wasting no time, he began to undo the straps that held the canvas and poles, dumped the gear on the ground, and at last brought out a large canteen of water.

The girl drank thankfully and, as she did so, Elliot looked past her to the body of the dead man and noted with disgust that the ravens had taken one of the eyes, leaving a bloody socket in its place. He knew that he must get the girl away from here, even if he could only manage to carry her a few hundred yards. His gaze moved back to the camping gear, spread out on the rough grass, and an idea began to form.

'What happened?' Her voice was faint but insistent. 'What happened to me? What am I doing here?'

He explained in as few words as possible but when he mentioned Joe she gasped in dismay.

'Oh, God, poor Joe .... He was shot! Is he dead?' Her face collapsed in grief as Elliot nodded his head. 'It was all my fault! He did not want to come – he wanted to go back ... it was me ... I did it!'

'Listen, Miss Campbell, what happened to Joe wasn't really your fault. You couldn't know you would meet up with these murderin' coyotes. Lie back – try to get some rest.'

The idea had formed itself in his mind and he hurried over to the pile of gear. As he had already noticed, Miss Campbell believed in carrying plenty with her, and there was enough to make up three tents – one for her, one for Joe, and the other for a storage tent, to cover the provisions during the nights. Some of the poles were designed to fit together and where this was not possible, he bound them with cord. In the end, he had made two long poles from the six short ones. He fitted the ends of these to the saddle of the pack horse and between them and where they trailed behind with their lower ends on the ground, he stretched the canvas, so as to form a rough stretcher, in imitation of an Indian travois.

The girl winced and twisted her face in pain as he lifted her on to the canvas. He made her as comfortable and secure as possible and then loaded the rest of the gear between both horses and led them slowly through the scrub and boulders towards the old trail. The mist had risen and the early sun was slanting long shadows by the time he reached the beaten track and turned back on the way he had come on the previous day. They made tortuous progress with the pole ends dragging stubbornly and jamming themselves every few yards amid the stones. Time after time, Elliot was forced to dismount to free them and to check that they were still bound securely. Even in these stretches where the trail widened a little, they could move at no greater pace than a slow walk.

He was aware that he had never before felt so vulnerable. If Proctor caught up with them now, the first knowledge that Elliot was likely to have of it would be a bullet in the back, and even if he saw or heard them coming, he would have no chance as he could not leave the girl to take cover or make his escape.

These morning hours dragged by, however, without any suggestion of such danger and gradually he began to feel that he was slowly but surely putting distance between himself and the gang. It seemed to him that if Proctor had been in serious pursuit, he could not have failed to make up upon them by this time. He chewed over the possible reasons for this in his mind but could come to no satisfactory conclusion. It could be, though, that it had something to do with that shot in the still hours of the night – if it was real and not imaginary – and, he felt almost convinced, something to do also with the Cheyenne, Half Yellow Face, on his war-path to seek his revenge and unmistakable in his war-paint ....

About halfway through the forenoon, Elliot decided to halt in the shade of a gigantic boulder. The girl needed to rest from the endless jolting of the rough journey and to push on relentlessly held, in these circumstances, more danger than to lose a little time. He built a small fire and made hot coffee for the first time in several days. The girl drank gratefully and seemed the better for it. Her mind was still overwhelmed, however, by grief for Joe and by a sense of guilt for her own foolhardiness in persuading him to go on into possible danger instead of taking his advice and making for home.

'I should have turned back after you warned me, Chris, but when you said that Jem had been kidnapped I just felt that I had to come after you. I thought maybe, between us, we could talk to these men ... and my father, being who he is, perhaps they would listen. Perhaps do some kind of a deal.' She saddened further as he shook his head. 'Oh, I know now that it was silly, Chris, but at the time ....'

'You only did what you thought was right, Miss Campbell, can't really blame yourself for that.'

He looked into the fire, sipping thoughtfully at his coffee. Somebody had told him once, a long time ago, that the road to hell was paved with good intentions and, many a time, he had felt it to be true. You do your best to sort something out and end up by making more of a mess out of it than it was at the start.

'Chris.' Her voice interrupted his reflections. Her tone held great sympathy and a hesitation, as if she was afraid to probe too deeply into his feelings. 'Chris, after we started to follow you, we heard ... well, we met an old squaw woman. She said that ... that Cra ... that Jem was dead. Is that correct, Chris? We didn't know whether to believe it or not.'

'It's true. He is dead.' Elliot's voice grew thick in a mixture of grief and anger. 'He was murdered. He was ... well, they murdered him.'

He could see no point in distressing her further with the grim details and he was not sure, in any case, if he could trust himself to speak of it any more. Not right now, anyway. He got up and walked away from her for a short distance. His eyes, as he looked back along the trail they had come, glistened with a weakness which, a week before, he would not have believed himself capable of. Moments passed before he regained control of himself and grief gave way, once again, to anger. Just then, he felt that he would have rejoiced to see Proctor and his men ride round that bend so that he could fight them to the finish but he knew, even as the thought came into his mind, how desperate he would be to defend the girl and how dismayed he would feel in his failure to do so.

When he returned to her, the girl said only two things – how sorry she was to hear about Jem's death and how aware she was that she owed her life to Elliot. After that, they both fell into a silence which lasted much of the day.

That night, having covered only about half the distance that they would normally have on horseback, they made camp by the trail. Elliot rigged up a little shelter for the girl, using spare canvas from one of the tents, and settled down to sleep some distance away so as to give her as much privacy as possible. Before sleeping, though, he cooked the best meal he had tasted in days, using some of the provisions Joe and she had carried. Such sleep as he had, though, was brief, and he lay awake most of the long night, his mind a turmoil of thought and emotion.

In the morning, he found the girl to be in much pain. Her face was white and drawn after a sleepless night.

'What's wrong, Miss Julie, is your head bad?' His voice was anxious, genuinely concerned.

'My head's just aching. That's all. It's my arm.' She grimaced in renewed pain. 'It's been torture. All night long.'

They both looked at the mess of twigs and rags. Suddenly she seemed to thrust her torment aside for a moment as she smiled impishly.

'What's that supposed to be anyway? Something that's fallen off an Egyptian mummy or a rat's nest?'

He looked at her sharply, surprised at her little sparkle of humour. Then he shrugged his shoulders, feeling some embarrassment.

'It was dark, Miss Julie, and I couldn't find anythin'.' He looked closely and seriously at the arm. 'Since you're gettin' all that pain, though, maybe we oughta look at it again.'

'It feels like it.' Her voice was again weary and pain-ridden and she spoke in hesitant gasps between spasms. 'But if you haven't ... thrown away too much ... of my property ... you should find a bandage ... some ointment ... in the baggage. Father always said we should carry them.' Again, came the flicker of a smile. 'In case of ... accidents.'

After some rummaging, he found the bandage and the ointment and a piece of flat wood that might have been intended for an emergency splint. When he took away the rags and twigs from her arm, he saw that she had suffered from the cloth being bound too tightly but, worse than that, the break in her upper arm was badly set and he could see the lump in her pink flesh where the bone was pushing its way out.

'That must be real sore, Miss Campbell,' he said, almost under his breath.

'I can't argue with that.' Her mouth was twisted again in pain.

'I'm sorry – but I think I'm goin' to have to try and set it again. We can't leave it like that, even for a few days.'

'I know.'

'I'm sorry – but it's goin' to be pretty painful.'

'I know that too.'

He rolled up her neckerchief and put it in her mouth so that she would have something to bite on. He gripped her arm above and below the break and then pulled firmly until he felt the bone grate into position. The girl stiffened in a muffled scream and thrashed the ground

with her free hand. Then she fell back, face white and
tense, eyes closed. Elliot put the splint carefully into
position and bandaged the arm as tenderly as he could.

After a few minutes, she opened her eyes with an
expression which told him that the pain, although still
severe, was not as savage as before.

'What about a little coffee, Miss Julie? Think you can
manage that?'

'As long as you don't expect me to make it ...!' She
smiled at him again in her good-humoured but faintly
ironic way, and as he turned to crawl out through the
tent door, he was amazed to hear her voice change to the
accents of a low-down cow-poke. 'Know somethin',
partner, yo' sho' am one helluva hoss doctor!'

He paused in his progress through the door, and,
without meaning at all to express his thoughts, replied,
'And you sure have guts, Julie. Nobody could argue with
that!'

She slept for much of the morning and he did not
disturb her, anxious as he was to press on. When they at
last got on to the trail again, it was the same slow
progress but now she engaged him almost constantly in
conversation, and although he was not, at first, in any
mood for talk, he gradually found himself playing his
part and his troubles moving a little from the forefront
of his mind.

Sometime the following day, they passed by the shack
in which Jem had died, Elliot tense and bitter, his anger
and despair welling up inside him. She fell silent too but
the next morning said that she thought that she might
be able to ride and they could then make better
progress. After some false attempts, she managed to
mount the pack horse and they left the clumsy and
collapsing travois behind and rode on at no great pace
but with the rising hope that their journey would soon
be at an end.

It happened just a little earlier than they had
anticipated. They were moving slowly down the lower

slopes of the old gold trail, when they saw a group of horsemen approaching them. There were three Indians and two whites. The man at the front was tall, dark moustached, and rode a handsome black stallion. Julie reined in the weary pack horse.

'That's my father!' Her voice was excited, relieved. 'It's Father!'

The meeting between father and daughter was an emotional one. Campbell, strong man though he was, had tears in his eyes. Julie embraced him as best she could with her one free arm and then told him all that had happened, detailing Elliot's part in her rescue. Campbell came forward and pressed Elliot by the hand.

'I've been looking around for my daughter for the past three days, ever since the Absarokee brought in Jem.' He looked at Elliot searchingly, as if attempting to sound out the depths of his feelings. 'Thank you for saving my daughter, Mr Elliot. There is no way that I can repay you ... I'm sorry about your brother. We gave him a decent burial. You can see his grave when we get back ....'

He broke off, seeing the expression in Elliot's eyes. Julie saw it too and the joy in her face was replaced by troubled anxiety. Elliot was silent for a moment, then began to turn his mount around.

'Thanks, Mr Campbell, for what you did for Jem ... but I can't go back now. I got somethin' else to do. I gotta go now.'

'Chris,' Campbell put out an arm as if to restrain him. 'You can't go after these men by yourself. You'll have no chance. Leave it to the law.'

'The law?' Elliot's tone was sardonic.

'I sent a man into Red Creek as soon as I could, so that Mulligan could round up a posse. Should have been out this way by this time but they'll be here before long. Anyhow, it is a job for the law, Chris. You can't go it alone.'

Elliot shook his head. It was true that under pressure

from an important man like Campbell, Mulligan would feel that he had to do something. Probably, he would round up a posse, but it would be slow, it would be inefficient, it would never get these men and that would suit Mulligan, who would rather let these renegades slip away than be forced to face them. It was true, also, that Campbell knew about Mulligan but, as the Indian Agent, he had to be seen to do things by the book – at least, now that his daughter was out of danger.

'I'm goin'.' Elliot spoke flatly, in a tone that brooked no further argument. 'They murdered my kid brother.'

Julie came up to him and, before he was aware of it, held his hand in her own. Her voice trembled a little as she spoke.

'Don't do it, Chris. It's madness. You'll just get yourself ....'

He looked into her dark eyes. They were soft, imploring. For a brief moment, he felt confused, then he withdrew his hand.

'I'm sorry, Julie, but I have to go.'

He turned away then but had not ridden any distance when Campbell caught up with him.

'All right, Chris, I can see you've made up your mind but, since you're determined, you'd better go as well prepared as you can. That dead-beat nag will only put you at a disadvantage. Take Prince. He's young and strong. Come on now – I insist! And take this hand-gun too – that worn out old Colt will only let you down. I'm sorry, I don't have a rifle to give you.'

'It's OK. I'm used to this rifle. Might not handle another one so well.'

'And what about provisions, Chris? Come on, as an old army man, you should know not to set out in such a hurry!'

Elliot saw the sense of the argument. He was doing this for Jem, he told himself, so he had no right not to give himself every chance of success. A few minutes later he was riding off on the black stallion, with Campbell's side-gun and belt of ammunition, and fresh provisions in his saddle-bag. Not far away, the rugged hills beckoned and taunted him, seeming to throw out a challenge to mortal combat, which he could not refuse, however little he rated his chances of survival.

He had not gone far when he heard Julie call out. 'Good luck, Chris!'

He waved an arm, without turning around to look at her. Her voice rang out again with the same ironic humour he had come to recognize but this time it held something else too – something that sounded like an entreaty.

'You make sure you bring my Pappy's hoss back now ... you hear me?'

Elliot rode on, wondering what it was that nagged and gnawed at his insides like a prairie dog.

SEVEN

He passed by Joe's remains, torn and scattered by scavengers, and held his breath at the stench. He rode over the pass with caution and eventually went by the camp he had detected from the far-off hill. There was no recent sign of them there either and his mind, filled to drowning point with the bitter waters of his grief and anger, sank into despair. It seemed to him that he must be now too late and the leaden blade in his heart turned once more in his belief that Jem must go unavenged and that the knowledge could never leave him.

He was riding through a narrow ravine, with his eyes scanning the rocky ledges all around, when the Cheyenne arrow dropped into the ground ahead of him. He pulled up the black stallion and stood still as the Indian wended his way down the steep slope, with a slight avalanche of scree under his pony's hooves, and approached with calm dignity.

The Cheyenne looked at Elliot for some moments in silence. The black war-paint of his forehead was torn by grazed skin. There was a smear of blood on his buckskin shirt and from his rough Indian saddle there hung a bloody scalp of straggling red hair. There was a weariness about him but it was physical tiredness only, for his dark eyes were still lit with fire and when he spoke it was with quiet confidence.

'I saw you come, Horse Soldier.' He smiled faintly at the flicker of surprise which crossed Elliot's face on hearing the term which had not been applied to him in years. 'Men close ahead. Do not ride into their bullets.'

Elliot stiffened in the saddle, his heart beginning to thump wildly. So, it was not too late! With the excitement of the prospect of action there came, however, the steadying hand of prudence.

'How near are they?'

The Cheyenne held his hands close together.

'You must leave this trail. The eyes are open.' As he spoke, he looked admiringly over the stallion and then questioningly at Elliot. 'The woman is safe?'

'She is with her father. He took her home. She should be OK.'

'Father give big present.'

'He lent me the horse,' grunted Elliot, irritated for some reason he could not understand. The Indian looked mystified but then dropped the subject as unimportant.

'Come.' Half Yellow Face leaned down from his pony to retrieve the arrow which had dropped into the trail. He then motioned Elliot to follow and rode off to one side, moving over rock-hard ground and looking back constantly to make certain that they were leaving no tracks likely to be seen by white men. From time to time, he signalled for Elliot to move on ahead, while he swept the dirt behind them with a long twig which he obviously carried for that purpose.

After some time, he paid less attention to covering their tracks and led the way at as quick a pace as the rough country made possible. They kept to no beaten path but wended their way amongst rocks and escarpments and through narrow, twisting ravines, until Elliot became convinced, experienced scout and trail-blazer though he was, that he would have had the greatest difficulty in finding his way back unaided.

At all times, the Cheyenne kept strict silence and communicated only by signs. Eventually, they reached a spot nearby the long dried-out bed of an ancient stream, which was partly concealed by stunted trees, gnarled and disfigured by mountain winds and arid soil. He seemed to be familiar with the place and, to judge by the flattened earth beneath the branches, had rested here more than once.

They dismounted and drank tepid water from Elliot's canteen and ate a little biscuit and pemmican. Elliot had been given a small quantity of oats for the stallion and these were shared out between both animals. The Indian munched contentedly for a few minutes before he spoke.

'You want fight men?' Elliot nodded in reply and the Cheyenne continued, 'I take you to men. You see. Then you fight.' He looked directly into Elliot's eyes. 'We fight.'

'We fight. Where are these men?'

The Cheyenne pointed across the rugged landscape, almost as if Proctor and his men were within view.

'How do you know they're still there?'

'They look all time. Look in ground for gold.'

Elliot sat up straight.

'The gold you told Jem about? What did ya tell him about the gold anyway?'

The Cheyenne gazed for a moment into the branches of the trees before replying.

'Crazy Man sits in the hand of Manitou. The ear listens.' He was again silent and then turned his gaze once more upon Elliot. 'You see Absarokee? Near? Far?'

Elliot understood the anxiety which underlay the question, although Half Yellow Face had asked in a tone which was calm and seemingly untroubled. Although the Absarokee were now tame Indians as far as the whites were concerned, the old feuds with other tribes such as the Cheyenne still smouldered on and it was apparent to Elliot that his companion knew himself to be in danger from that quarter as well as from Proctor's gang.

'I saw some of them, days ago, where the old gold road turns around the bluff, but they were goin' away ...

towards Red Creek.' They were silent for some minutes then Elliot spoke again. 'Proctor – the white bandits didn't come t'kill me when I was left with the white woman. Why was that?'

The Cheyenne's eyes were flat and expressionless.

'They see Half Yellow Face. Yellow Face like gold picture.'

Elliot had guessed as much but having his guess confirmed told him something more about his new ally. The Cheyenne had known that Proctor could not fail to recognize him in his war-paint and greed for the gold would lead him into attempting to capture the Indian instead of investigating the shots he must have heard that evening. So the Indian had drawn off Proctor and his men, at great danger to himself, though whether he had done this for Elliot or the woman or from some sense of honour or bravado, it was not possible to judge with certainty.

When the sun had moved further across the sky, sending deep shadows into the gullies and down the rock chasms, they left the horses where they were and climbed by a devious route through the boulders and shifting stones and scree until they reached a high point, where the Cheyenne motioned that they should crawl forward, keeping as low as possible. Within a further few minutes, they found themselves looking down into a deep ravine, much of which was still hidden from view from where they lay.

At first, Elliot saw nothing of significance but then the tiny figure of a man came into sight, moving slowly, with his head bent forward and stopping every few feet to scrape at the soil or pull a stone to one side, all of his attention, apparently, taken up with the search. Elliot did not believe that he had ever seen the man before but then he felt his fingers tense upon the sharp rock as the dark-clothed figure of Wilson appeared, also searching, but straightening up frequently and looking around with an expression of deepening impatience and irritation. A moment later, the head and shoulders of Proctor could also be seen and his voice heard, raised in anger. Several other voices joined in, indistinct, muffled but full of rage. The argument continued for some minutes and only gradually subsided as Half Yellow Face drew Elliot back from the edge.

When they had returned to their camping place, which they reached in a surprisingly short time, the Cheyenne expressed what was already in Elliot's mind.

'Men look for gold two-three days. They tired. They speak angry. Soon they go. We fight when sun reach sky.'

They settled down where they were to sleep. The Indian lay down on the bare earth and seemed to fall asleep instantly, his breathing almost silent, and scarcely stirred during the entire night, although some part of his senses remained alert enough to cause him to open his eyes once when an owl flew over and again, much, later, at the cry of a distant wolf. Elliot was not so fortunate. The excitement of the prospect of the rapidly approaching conflict and the desire to avenge the death of Jem again seethed through his mind, and he lay awake for hours in the darkness, while the wind whistled through the canyons.

They were up before light and Half Yellow Face led the way partly along the route they had taken on the previous day but then cut off through a series of narrow passes. Although the terrain was unfamiliar to Elliot, he knew well enough where they were headed. The canyon in which Proctor and his gang were searching was Dead Mouth. That much he knew from its depth and shape and from a sighting he had had of it as a boy. He knew also that it had only one mouth and, after a mile or so, reached a dead end. There was only one way in – and you could only leave the same way – the way you came in …. The obvious and the only possible plan was to take up a position at the entrance and ambush these outlaws as they attempted to leave. When they would decide to leave, it was not possible to say, but the Cheyenne expected it to be soon, and if they did not leave when expected, then they would both wait patiently until their chance came.

The sun was well up as they approached the narrow entrance, dismounted and then went forward, with extreme caution, on foot. They moved slowly and silently from cover to cover, taking advantage of every stone, bush and shadow. Suddenly, the Cheyenne halted and raised a hand in quiet warning. Peering from behind a sheltering boulder, Elliot followed his line of vision and made out the form of a man, seated part of the way up one side of the canyon, his body partly shielded by a large rock. He was slouched forward, elbows on knees, his whole demeanour one of boredom or indolence. He was evidently a sentry, positioned to give warning of any approach to the mouth of the canyon, but weary of his task and impatient to be relieved by one of his companions.

Half Yellow Face crouched and stretched out the long barrel of his ancient rifle along the surface of a stone. He held the firearm steady and took slow and careful aim. The head, chest and part of the legs of the sentry were all clearly visible and the man was stationary, making no more movement than to scratch a limb or swat at an irritating fly. It was an easy target and Elliot held his breath as he waited for the execution to take place ....

The Cheyenne pulled the trigger. The gun roared and the bullet missed by about a yard, struck a ledge of rock and ricochetted up the slope.

For a brief moment, the man seemed transfixed with amazement, then he leapt from his perch to the nearest cover. Elliot could see part of his head shifting from side to side, as he tried to discover where the shot had come from, and a hand holding a six-gun, ready to retaliate. A moment passed, then the sentry turned and started into a low, crouching run towards his horse, tethered a short distance further into the canyon.

As soon as the man moved, Half Yellow Face stood up, fitted an arrow rapidly into his bow, and released it. The bow sang and the arrow found its mark, burying itself into the outlaw's lower back. His legs collapsed under him, he twisted round in anguish and broke off the shaft while blood spurted over back and hand. For a second, he seemed unable to rise, then he struggled up and stumbled on. He had almost reached the horse, when Elliot fired and struck him between the shoulder blades. With a cry the man pitched to the ground and lay still.

Elliot hesitated, half expecting the outlaw to make another attempt to move, and then looked around for Half Yellow Face. To his surprise, the Cheyenne was not to be seen. Elliot sank back behind the cover of the large boulder and, as he did so, saw the Indian go past at the gallop, having run back to mount his pony. As he went by the inert form of the sentry, Half Yellow Face hung low over his pony's neck and struck at the man with his bow. It seemed a wild, crazy action but Elliot knew that the Cheyenne was counting coup, which – to the Indian mind – was almost as important as killing the enemy. He did not stop at that, however, but continued with the next part of his plan, which was to gallop on around a bend and disappear from view.

Elliot lay in wait as he heard shouting, a shot and the galloping of hooves. Half Yellow Face appeared again, going flat out and followed, a few moments later, by a bunch of horsemen. In the cloud of dust, Elliot made out that there were four, two almost neck and neck at the front, a third shortly behind the first two, and another, darkly clad, some way to the rear. He had little time for observation but recognized Proctor as one of the riders at the head and raised his rifle to fire. He took swift but careful aim but, just before he pulled the trigger, the other leading rider drew slightly forward and took the bullet intended for the gang boss. It slammed into his body and the impact threw him sideways from the saddle and into Proctor.

Both fell to the ground amid the milling hooves of the frightened animals. The man who was hit remained in a crumpled heap but Proctor jerked desperately to his feet and threw himself into the nearest piece of cover on the same side of the gorge as Elliot had fired from.

Behind this mêlée, Billy Wolf drew sharp rein on his pony, turned it to the other side and leapt from the saddle. Before Elliot could draw a bead on him, he had taken refuge in thick scrub and vanished from sight. Still further back, the dark-clothed rider, now recognizable as Wilson, turned his horse aside into a clump of elder.

Elliot raised himself up slightly and strained to catch a glimpse of Proctor. For some minutes there was no sign of him, then he could be seen crawling and clambering up the slope, keeping his head down as far as possible, but obviously intending to reach some point further up from which he could shoot down on Elliot's position. For some moments, the intervening rocks and bushes gave no chance of getting in a worthwhile shot as Proctor was smart enough to take full advantage of every scrap of cover he could get. At last, though, he reached a ledge where the cover ran out but from which he could get a fair view of Elliot's head and shoulders.

It was here that his common sense and his luck ran out. Thinking himself not to have been seen climbing the slope, and believing he could get in a couple of quick shots, he hauled himself on to the ledge, stood up and turned around, his finger already tightening on the trigger ....

Elliot, though, was ready for him. The cavalry rifle bullet gouged into the centre of Proctor's face, tearing open a great hole where his nose had been, and exploded through the back of his skull, spattering blood, brains and bone across the rock wall behind him. His heels slipped and dug two furrows into the earth just under the ledge. He toppled sideways and fell, arms flailing in a wild circular movement, shattered head spewing blood, and rolled, thumping and pounding, until his broken corpse sprawled amongst the boulders at the base of the slope.

'Christ!' The voice, barely recognizable as that of Wilson, yelled out in horror. 'Proctor's got it!'

For some minutes there was silence, broken only by the bewildered neighing and stamping of the loose horses. Elliot reloaded and scanned the opposite side of the gorge for any sign of the half-breed. For a while, he could see nothing but then he made out a trace of the black hat with its white feather edging its way through the scrub. It was gradually moving upwards, as if propelled by the same idea that had possessed Proctor, but with infinitely more care and caution.

He looked around for the Cheyenne and saw him advancing slowly at an angle up the side of the gorge almost opposite to himself, bent double, as if stalking a wild animal. Half-breed and Indian were both intent on the same deadly purpose, vying with one another for some advantage in the coming combat. To his dismay, Elliot saw that Half Yellow Face still carried his long rifle, in which he evidently retained supreme confidence. As he watched, he observed the Indian stop and crouch down over the weapon, as if attempting to load it or adjust some part of its ancient mechanism. It seemed that the half-breed also noticed or guessed at the action for he suddenly bounded from his shelter in the boulders to the cover of a thicket, which would enable him to approach quite close to the Cheyenne without exposing himself to Elliot's rifle.

Elliot was in two minds whether to take a shot into the bush in the hope of striking lucky, when he saw Half Yellow Face raise the gun and point it in the direction where Elliot guessed the half-breed was likely to be. It seemed that the Cheyenne's preoccupation with loading might just have been a ruse to tempt Billy Wolf into showing himself as he moved in to attack what he thought was an unprepared opponent. Elliot, from

where he was, could not see the half-breed but it was
evident that the Indian could and was about to shoot
him down ....

Then there came the sound of a thunder clap and the
teeth-rending shrill of tearing metal as the breech of the
old gun exploded. Half Yellow Face reeled back, hands
up and outspread, head jolted to one side. He slid some
feet down the slope, his shattered rifle clattering
alongside him.

In that instant, Billy Wolf heard and understood. He
leapt from the thicket and raised his revolver to destroy
the helpless Cheyenne at close range. It would only take
one quick shot and then he could drop again into cover.
His Colt .45 trained itself on the Indian's heart but then
jerked up as Elliot's bullet tore across the half-breed's
chest, ripping out a strip of skin and surface flesh.

Billy Wolf fell to his knees, with the blood pouring
into his buckskin shirt and down through the hair of his
belly. His face twisted in pain but through the mist
which floated for a moment before his eyes, he made
out Elliot on the other side of the gorge. He clenched his
teeth and fired off two shots but the range was just too
much for the Colt to be effective and so he turned and
crawled like an angry, wounded beast back into hiding,
fearful of a second rifle bullet.

At that, Elliot sprang up and ran across the open
space between himself and the stricken Cheyenne. He
had no sooner reached the Indian's side, than the dark
form of Wilson thundered by, anxious to escape from
the trap that the ravine now was. Elliot whirled around
and fired but it was too late and, although he thought he
saw Wilson jerk in the saddle, he felt that it was unlikely
that he had scored a hit.

The Cheyenne was sitting up, shaking his head as if to
clear it. Elliot saw that he had a red scorch mark across
his face and the palms of his hands were blistering.
Luckily, his eyes had escaped injury and he did not seem
to be otherwise hurt.

'You're damn lucky ya didn't git all your fingers blown off,' growled Elliot. 'Foolin' around with that goddamn beat-up old rifle.'

The Cheyenne made no answer but his eyes suddenly changed expression as he looked past Elliot's shoulder. Elliot turned in time to see Billy Wolf mount up on his pony, jittery and scared in the confusion, and tug its head around and force it towards them at speed. The half-breed's shirt was a mass of blood and he swayed almost drunkenly in the saddle, but he galloped down upon them, loosening off shots as he came. A slug struck the ground within inches of Elliot's foot, another buzzed past his ear. He rolled to one side and stood up, swinging his rifle by the barrel.

Billy Wolf pressed his pony to move nearer to them but the beast balked at the bouldered slope facing it and turned away. Billy Wolf twisted to get in another shot but Elliot struck hard with the butt of the rifle against the half-breed's upper left arm and shoulder and almost knocked him to the ground. The pony capered round in terror while Billy hung on desperately. He regained control but now the pain in his arm, the blood pouring from his wound – the gravity of which he was uncertain – and the realization that he was on his own, all combined to take the fight out of him, and he pressed the spurs of his high boots into his crazed steed and made off out of the ravine before Elliot could begin to reload.

For a few moments they waited in silence, finding it difficult to comprehend that the danger seemed, for the present, to be over. Then they went back for the black stallion and the skewbald pony, mounted up, and moved slowly into the mouth of the canyon. Neither felt like taking off immediately in pursuit. Half Yellow Face was still shaken. Elliot seemed suddenly drained of energy. Nothing was said but both understood that things were not finished – the act of revenge was incomplete, the war-path not yet fully trodden ....

Some feeling of curiosity made Elliot look down at the man he had shot from the saddle. He was stockily built, balding slightly and had an old scar on his forehead. He lay in a pool of blood from his bullet wound and one hand was crumpled and broken from a horse's hoof. A short distance away the man who had been on look-out also lay, but now, strangely, twisted half round on his back instead of flat on his face. As they drew near, they heard him groan.

As they bent over him, they saw that his eyes were half-closed, clouded and dying, but he appeared to become aware of their presence and opened his mouth as if to speak. Elliot slid from the saddle to listen, not out of pity, but from that feeling that the words of a dying man should be listened to.

'Gawd.' The voice was harsh, croaking through blood. 'Elliot ... ain't it? You're Elliot ... goofy guy's brother ....'

Elliot felt his heart turn to ice. He struck the man across the face with the palm of his hand but the outlaw seemed not to feel the blow although he sensed the anger.

'Don't mean nothin' .... Didn't mean no harm.' His speech was disjointed, interrupted by fits of coughing. 'Didn't mean t'kill the kid ... kinda accident.'

'Accident ...?'

'Yeah. Wasn't really meant. See, Wilson allus hated the kid. Reckoned he was allus laughin' at him 'cause o' you knocking him down in the street that day ... then Wilson starts to ... starts to punch the kid around. Shoves him inta the shack. Then he says thet the goo ... thet the kid knows helluva lot more 'bout thet gold than he was makin' out an' thet he was gonna scare hell outa him to make'm talk .... So he ... so he ties his hands and puts him up on the box 'n puts rope aroun' his neck and says to leave'm there till he was ready to tell us somethin' 'bout the gold .... Then we goes outside t' light the fire 'n get coffee ... an' then we finds ... Pulley finds some ole hoss shoes an' we starts slingin' them around and kinda

forgit about the kid ... Then Proctor comes back an'
when we goes back inta the shack the kid's dead. Hung
'isself. Kicked away the goddamned box. Shoulda stayed
still. He'd a' been OK if he'd stayed still. But he was
hung .... Then there was one helluva row. Proctor says
we flung away 'bout the only good card we got ... an'
Billy ... Christ, Billy was near goin' crazy, he was so mad!
Billy was near drawin' on Wilson an' Pulley an' me ....
But then Proctor says it didn't make no sense fightin'
among ourselves an' the best thing we could do was t'
forgit it an' t' move along the trail aways t' make a new
camp .... Kid ... shoulda stayed still. Why'n hell he hafta
kick away the goddamned box ...?'

Elliot's eyes were closed. His body was tense. In his
mind, he could feel Jem's fear. The rope – the
darkening shack – the feeling of being alone, deserted.
The pain of the beating he had endured, the cord
tightening around his neck, the helplessness of his
bound hands, the terror, the panic, the frenzied kicking
out .... Then the terrible agony of strangulation and the
waves of death pouring into his brain, sweeping him
into the darkness. ... and all the time, his voice calling
helplessly, hopelessly, silently ... Chris! Chris! Where
was Chris ...?

How long he remained crouching in the dirt Elliot did
not know but when he regained his senses and an
awareness of his surroundings he saw that the Cheyenne
had killed the man with his knife and was cutting and
tearing the scalp, while the blood dribbled down the
dead face ....

EIGHT

They had rested a little and ate and drank a little and felt the better for it. Now they were on their way out of the ravine and Half Yellow Face picked up the trail of Billy Wolf and Wilson with little difficulty although the ground was hard and dry. How long these conditions would remain, it was hard to say as clouds were gathering once more from the west and the gnarled trees and clumps of elder swayed and tossed in the rising breeze.

Every few yards, the Cheyenne saw a spot of blood and, after a number of miles, they came to a place where there was more of it – a spattering and a tiny, drying-out pool, as if the half-breed had been forced to stop to take time to bind up his wound in some manner. After that, there were no more such spots on the trail.

Later, they arrived at the place where the two outlaws had met up again with one another as their tracks converged and the ground was trampled where the horses had stood and stamped restlessly as the riders had spoken.

Elliot wondered what had been said. He could imagine Billy Wolf's voice raised in anger at his desertion and Wilson's defensive argument. Then they would have to decide on the next move. To stand and fight somewhere along the trail or to give up altogether and ride like hell out of the territory? Maybe they would decide to go since they had not found the hiding place of the gold and there seemed little prospect that they would. On the other hand, anger and resentment might persuade them to lie in ambush so as to put paid to Elliot and the Cheyenne. After all, it was still a fair enough contest. Two white men – well just about – armed with Colts against one man armed with an old rifle and an Indian with a bow and arrows ...

But would they think it worth the risk? What was there to be gained from fighting? And again, to judge by what he had seen and heard, Elliot felt convinced that there was no sense of comradeship or mutual regard between these two. The gang had seemed to be losing its cohesion even before this disastrous morning and now they must be sickened and despairing and maybe each man thinking only of himself; and, again, the half-breed was wounded, though possibly not seriously ....

For his own part, Elliot was calm and self-possessed. The terrible flood of sorrow and anger that had poured through him had vanished like a pool left by a sudden cloudburst in the desert. His deep emotions were buried and in their place was a hard resilience, as a scab forms across a wound.

For the remaining part of the forenoon they made good progress as the Cheyenne, even in these unfavourable conditions, seemed to know at what speed the horses ahead were travelling and pushed his own pony to keep pace and, at times, where the route was obvious, moved at a speed designed to overtake.

A little later in the day, the clouds thickened and a little rain began to fall. As they went on, the tracks became clearer in the light mud but they were both well aware that a prolonged and heavy downpour, if it came, could ruin their hopes of ever catching up by washing out the tracks almost as soon as they were made.

Half Yellow Face was no conversationalist, as Elliot had quickly learned and appreciated as a quality which he, himself, was perfectly at ease with, but, as the day wore on, he became aware that this natural reserve was giving way to something else. The Cheyenne's mood changed by degrees from a quiet optimism to a thoughtful and pessimistic air. He began to urge his pony less and, at times, he drew almost to a halt and seemed to look, unseeing, into the sky or the red sandstone or into the mixed pebbles of the trail, as if the clouds which were darkening the sky were also darkening his mind. For a long time, Elliot made no comment but eventually he spoke.

'You OK, Half Yeller Face? Hands burnin' maybe?'

The Indian's hands had blistered from the accident with the gun but so far he had not minded, or had chosen to ignore the pain.

'Hands?' The Cheyenne looked almost surprised at the suggestion and shook his head. But he looked at his palms and fingers in the same thoughtful manner.

'Horse Soldier.' His voice was heavy with a growing despair. 'Gun try to kill Half Yellow Face.'

'Eh? What d'ya mean? You pulled the trigger. The gun burst. It was an old gun. Ya shouldn't have been usin' it at all. You was lucky!'

The Cheyenne shook his head once more.

'This gun – gift from Father. Always good medicine in war. Now shoot Half Yellow Face. Maybe spirit angry. Father Spirit angry.'

'Now look here.' Elliot tried not to smile. 'A rusty old gun ain't much use. It can't last forever. Nothin' lasts forever. You know that. How many times you had to change that bowstring? Your moccasins never wear out? You'll hafta change that buckskin shirt of yours pretty soon too ….'

The Cheyenne stared in astonishment at his lack of understanding.

'Gun always good medicine from Father.'

Elliot hesitated, seeing the gulf of incomprehension between them. The redskin believed firmly that it had been no ordinary gun. It was a valued gift from his father. Probably his father had used it for decades and it had proved its worth in war. It had magical qualities and had always shot at the enemy before, maybe more successfully in the hands of the father than in those of the son, but now it had turned against the son – and in the face of the enemy too – so what did that mean? Maybe the Father Spirit was angry. Elliot did not know what to say next. To argue white logic against Indian superstition and religious belief was a waste of time, and to attempt it could only give offence.

'Who was your father, Half Yellow Face ...?' He asked, and then his voice trailed off lamely as he remembered that the Cheyenne would not willingly mention the names of any of the dead of his own tribe for fear of giving offence to their spirits.

They followed along in the tracks of their quarry in silence. After more hours of riding, they found themselves emerging from the towering crags into a gentler landscape of hills, high and steep still, but less likely to provide cover for an easy ambush, which they had been looking out for all day. Here a narrow river was cutting out a valley for itself, sometimes broadening out a little but always swiftly flowing and creating rapids and tumbling rock-falls.

'Let's drink.' Elliot felt oddly pleased to break the long and dismal silence. 'We could do with it. The horses too.'

They crouched down at the river bank and tasted the delights of the cool fresh water after days of sipping from the canteen. Elliot was cupping his hand for another draught when he heard the Cheyenne gasp.

'Absarokee!'

Elliot swung round, his hand going for Campbell's gun at his hip. His fingers stopped at the butt, though, when he saw his companion staring at the pony. For a second, he was completely puzzled. The hill behind them seemed to hold no sign of Indians. Dark birds, ravens, winged overhead against the dark of the sky and one, he saw, had landed near the pony. In its sharp bill, it held something which it was attempting to rend to pieces before swallowing. A moment later, it flapped up and on to the Indian saddle with the object still dangling. Then Elliot realized what it carried and was trying to consume. It was a scalp ... a black-haired scalp, still bloody and hanging with remnants of human skin.

Elliot stared at the Cheyenne, who sat motionless, as if thunderstruck. The bird dropped the scalp and then tugged at the other, the red-haired one, still fastened to the front of the saddle, but, as Elliot straightened himself up, it rose, balanced itself in the stiffening breeze, and flapped off, empty billed, to the hillside.

'Absarokee.' The word came again, whispered and hoarse.

Elliot stood, silent and wondering, before half of the answer occurred to him. 'Absarokee' was an Indian word which he knew. In the dialects of some of the tribes the word 'absarokee' meant simply 'raven' and the tribal name came from the tribal totem, as was not unusual. So Half Yellow Face had seen the raven steal the scalp – but that could not explain such a reaction ....

Then Elliot saw the rest of the answer rising up before him; to the Cheyenne the totem represented the tribe, and here was the totem of his enemies tearing and destroying the scalps that were the fruits of his recent victories. It was another sign – a bad sign. Elliot felt his heart beginning to sink still further as some premonition of what was to come presented itself to his mind.

The Cheyenne had taken his medicine bag from his neck and had emptied out its contents. To Elliot it looked like so much rubbish – the tiny skull of some small animal, a piece of snake skin, a bright pebble, an old arrowhead .... These objects were moved about in what seemed a haphazard manner, then they were returned to the bag and the Cheyenne stood up.

'The war-path is ended. Half Yellow Face cannot kill Light Eyes or Black Coat. The spirits have said this. The Death Bear breathes on Half Yellow Face.'

'You can't mean that!' Elliot felt indignant and angry. 'We can't let these animals get away after what they've done! What about Jem? What about your friend, Jones?'

'The wise man turns when the earth opens in front of him. I must go to my people.'

'And leave these scum to ride out o' here! Look, we have a chance of catchin' up on them. Let's take it! We can't back down because of this ... this .... It don't make no sense. Anyhow, if you ain't goin', I am! If it's the last thing I do.'

He saw the uselessness of further argument. The Cheyenne, in his own mind, was not backing off for some trivial or unclear reason. He was stating what, to him, was a fact. There was no way he could kill these men. The spirits had said so, therefore it was a fact. So there was no use at all in trying – any more than there was any use in trying to fly in the air or fight a couple of grizzlies off with his bare hands.

The Cheyenne had already gone over to his pony. He tied the torn scalp on to his rough saddle and paused for a moment, as if deep in thought. He then went down to the stream and spent some minutes washing the black and the yellow ochre from his face, and watched the mixture of colour swirl away in the current. There seemed something symbolic in the act, and when he climbed back up the bank, the unsettled swirl of emotion had gone from him, and he was calm and resigned, as a man who has accepted a decision not of his own making.

He mounted his pony and turned in a small circle until he came to a halt beside Elliot.

'Horse Soldier, I must go to my people.'

'I know.' Elliot had no resentment. He knew that the Cheyenne was no coward and had no other motive than the one he had described. 'I reckon I understand you pretty well, Half Yeller Face.'

'Pray to your spirits, Horse Soldier.' ·

'Yeah. Maybe I'll do that.'

The Cheyenne seemed about to say something else but changed his mind. Instead, he drew one of the striped-feathered Cheyenne arrows from his quiver and passed it down to Elliot with an almost ceremonious gesture.

'The arrow flies straight. It will lead to the heart of your enemies.'

'Thanks.' Elliot smiled thinly. 'And thanks, too, for everythin' you've done.'

He watched as the Indian moved off back the way they had come, and then he walked, in deep thought, over to the black stallion, slipped the arrow under the strap of his saddle-bag, and mounted up.

The little valley gradually broadened to some extent and the banks of the river became grass and sedge covered. The trail left by the two outlaws was not seen now as the tracks of hooves but instead, as two wavering lines of bent, wet grass, flattened and arrowing in the direction they had travelled. It went on in this way for many miles and Elliot spurred his horse to greater efforts, anxious now to bring matters to a head.

As time went on, he became convinced that he was gaining on them, and this was confirmed when he saw two tiny dots in the distance, which grew larger by the minute. It seemed to him that they were moving slowly, probably because their horses were tired or maybe because they believed that they had put a long enough distance between themselves and their pursuers and were more confident as a result.

Some time after he set eyes upon them, however, he made out the far off white of a face, and knew that he, in turn, had been seen. They rode on more quickly then and disappeared over a rise, but later, he saw them again, and this time, he made out Billy Wolf with his pony at a standstill on a hillside, peering back to get a view of him.

So, they knew now that he was alone.

The realization came as no surprise. It was only to be expected and he had turned it over in his mind with calm consideration as he followed their trail through the miles of long grass. What they would do next would be to turn back towards him at some point, or, more likely, to lie in ambush where they had some cover, in the hope of getting close enough to him to be able to use their Colts without being shot down at a greater distance by the longer range and accuracy of the rifle. Once that happened, the dice would be heavily loaded against him.

Darkness began to close in and, with it, his senses became sharper and his nerves more tense. Overhead, the cloud cover was being ripped apart by the rising wind and the sun went down with only a flickering of red defiance behind the gloom of the hills. He knew that to ride on was to invite death.

Ahead of him, the river was turning itself on a wide bend. Along its banks were clumps of low trees and bushes and he stopped at a little grove and tethered the black stallion. On foot, he made his way along the banks and then, as the darkness became deeper, he turned away from the river and moved to the highest point of land he could find nearby, which was a little knoll which gave a view of the broad sweep of the river.

He settled down behind a heap of stones, made sure his rifle was at the ready and prepared for a long wait. As the darkness spread all around in the grass and trees, the moon began to show itself fitfully through gaps in the cloud. As he had anticipated, the river gleamed silver, and against it trees and bushes, growing along its banks, were silhouetted for brief moments and he knew that he would have a good chance of seeing any movement through the night, and would be able to shoot from the dark before they could get near to him.

The hours dragged on, though, and there was no sign of them. Slowly, the moon made her way over the sky, as he struggled to keep awake, fearful that a few minutes of sleep might cost him his life. In spite of that knowledge however, he did, in fact, doze off for brief spells, and always awoke apprehensive and angry at his own weakness.

The greyness of dawn came at last, and he got up

from the dew-sodden grass, stiff and cold and puzzled and went back to where the horse awaited him. He fed the stallion from his depleted bag of corn and then forced himself to light a fire and make hot coffee. The smoke from the damp wood rose into the morning air and could probably have been seen from far away but he did not care about that. They knew where he was, anyway, and since they had not attempted anything in the dark, they would not be likely to try it now.

As he drank the soothing, hot liquid, he wondered why they had not come. On the face of it, it looked as if they had decided that, since there was nothing to be gained from killing him, it made no sense to risk a rifle bullet and the best course of action was to try to shake him off and get well clear of the whole mess of a business as quickly as they could.

That meant that they would be making all speed from now on, and he would have to ride long and hard to catch up.

He picked up their tracks again, although they were much less clear after the long hours of the night had allowed the beaten-down grass to begin to straighten itself, and the trail seemed to follow along the banks of the river as they had done all the previous afternoon. As he rode, he kept a look-out for their campsite of the previous night but did not find it for many miles. Even then, it was clear to him, from the small area cropped by the horses, the lack of any ashes left by a fire, and the shallow depressions left by their bodies as they rested in the grass, that they had not paused for long. It looked as if they had ridden through most of the hours of darkness and had stopped to rest in the early morning before pushing on and leaving a much clearer trail through the dewy grass of the dawn.

So they were doing everything in their power to leave him behind. They were not out to ambush him but were only intent upon getting well away. Pretty soon, when conditions were more favourable, they would find ways of concealing their tracks and slowing him down, and, with reasonable luck, losing him altogether .... It was essential that he shorten the distance between them and himself before that could happen, and he had, he believed, one important advantage – he was better mounted, as the black stallion was stronger and swifter, he felt sure, than the inferior animals ridden by the men he was pursuing.

He spurred the horse on and made good time on the relatively flat ground and with a clear enough trail to follow. After a time, it became obvious to him that he was making up the ground he had lost the night before as the double trail of broken and bent blades became fresher by the hour. At about mid-morning, however, he saw something in the distance and slowed down to a trot ....

It was, he saw, a long stick, standing upright and, as he came nearer, he observed that its top was broken and hanging as if to make sure that it caught his attention. He approached cautiously and then drew to a halt beside a large boulder, half-hidden in the grass about twenty yards from the river bank. The broken length of branch was sticking into the earth beside it and all around, the grass had been trampled by their horses. What held his attention, though, was the boulder itself. The moss and lichen had been scraped from a large area of its surface and someone had taken a lump of soft sandstone and had scrawled out a message upon the tough granite in large, crude letters.

It read: *Elyit. Sorry bout the kid it was Wilson dun it. B.W.* and beside this scrawl, the shape of an arrow had been scraped out, pointing downriver, where the trail of a single horseman led off into the distance ....

Another track turned away to the west.

For a long time, Elliot stood, reading and rereading the rough message. Something about the crude, childish lettering carried with it a suggestion of sincerity. Maybe Billy Wolf was sorry about what had happened to Jem.

Sure enough, the dying man in the ravine had said that Billy was just about ready to draw on Wilson and the two others who had hanged Jem, and had also indicated that Wilson was the main culprit. Not that this could be seen as some kind of ridiculous apology for Billy Wolf's part in the course of events which had culminated in such a hideous crime. Billy Wolf had lingered behind long enough, after parting from Wilson, to scrape out this message for two other reasons: he reckoned that if Wilson got a rifle bullet in the back of the head it would be no more than he deserved – and he did not want Elliot picking up the wrong trail and following *him* ....

Elliot did not hold Billy Wolf blameless in the death of Jem. It was the half-breed, after all, who had kidnapped or led Jem off and into the clutches of the gang. In that he was guilty, and should be made to suffer for it. But he could not follow two trails at once and the hatred he felt for Wilson as the man who had beaten up Jem and put that rope around his neck, far outweighed all else and there was no real decision to be made as to which of the two outlaws he must get to grips with.

Wilson's trail along by the grass of the river bank was not hard to follow. It was impossible for any rider not to leave an obvious track in such conditions and Wilson kept a straight enough course as if he felt that it was more important to keep up his speed and put distance between himself and Elliot rather than to attempt time-wasting manoeuvres in probably futile efforts to shake him off.

After a time, the river flowed more slowly and eventually began to broaden out as it met with the waters of a lake. The margins were soggy and, at times, degenerated into stretches of marsh, so that Wilson's trail wound in a series of wide curves to avoid them. There were more stands of trees also, mostly willow and alder, and Elliot found himself slowing up as he was forced to approach these clumps of cover warily to prevent himself riding into a possible ambush.

It was when he was advancing carefully towards just such a small piece of woodland, with the sun high overhead, that he saw a movement on the outer edge of the trees at a point where they hung over a patch of swamp. He stopped and drew out his rifle, convinced for the moment that the time for the show-down with his enemy had arrived, but a very few minutes of observation told him that there were two riders coming through the trees, both on ponies and both Indian.

When they saw him, both came to a halt and stared in apparent apprehension. Then, as if in recognition of him, the leading rider held up an arm in greeting and urged his pony forward, followed, much more slowly, by the second.

As they came nearer, Elliot realized that they were the two young Absarokee who had surprised him at the miner's shack when he had been attempting to bury Jem. The young man at the front still had his buffalo lance hanging from the rough Indian saddle, but he also carried a light bow across his shoulders and a few arrows at his belt, of the kind used for hunting birds, lightly made and with hardened wood or bone points. A brace of wild duck hung from his pony's neck. The other youth was armed in the same way, though without a lance, but Elliot saw at once that he was injured, with a blood-soaked rag around his shoulder and he clung to his pony's neck as if weak and ill.

'What happened to your friend?' asked Elliot, as they approached.

The youth with the lance seemed nervous and agitated.

'White man shoot. White man shoot two, three, many times. No reason. Bullet strike Star Song ....'

'White man? What kind of a white man?'

The young man shrugged.

'White man ... black coat ... hairy nose. Wicked man.' His voice rose in indignation and anger. 'No reason to shoot. We have no gun. Cannot fight. We ride away through water.'

Elliot nodded thoughtfully. It was Wilson all right. It fitted the clear picture he had in his mind of Wilson to hear of him taking pot shots at unarmed Indian boys just for the malicious hell of it.

'Tell your friend to get down from the pony,' he said calmly. 'Let's look at that wound.'

The bullet had gone through the upper part of the boy's arm, tearing out flesh and muscle. The bleeding had almost ceased but Elliot could see that muscles had been destroyed, probably beyond hope of healing. The boy would almost certainly be crippled for life even if he could avoid the danger of gangrene.

Elliot bound up the wound again and gave the young man a drink from his canteen, as he seemed on the point of fainting.

'Soon as you get a chance,' he advised, 'boil up some water and make sure you keep that wound clean. Tie it up with a clean bit of cloth if you have any. Get home, quick as you can. Try to see Campbell. He'll fix him up better than you kin do in your village.'

The youth with the lance grunted and nodded as if accepting the advice with gratitude but Elliot could see that his mind was still afire with rage.

'Why did black-coat man shoot? Absarokee not fight white man! Our old chiefs have said this – Chief Campbell has said this!'

'I know ....'

'Absarokee are not afraid! We are not afraid to fight!' He seemed almost to be picking up their conversation from the day they had met at the shack but was now much more emotional and wild in his talk. 'Absarokee have always been warriors!'

'Yeah, I know ... I know. Listen, the best thing you kin do is get back to your people like I told you. Look after your friend real good. Here.' He turned to his saddle-bag and pulled out dried meat and some biscuit. 'Take this. I reckon you could do with it ... and here.' He felt that he wanted to say or do something that would help the boy to feel better about himself, boost his self-confidence in some way. 'Take this.' He drew the Cheyenne arrow from under the strap of the saddle-bag. 'The arrow flies straight. Right to the heart of your enemy! Could be good medicine.' He smiled good-humouredly and then became more serious. 'And, who knows? Maybe you and your people will get a square deal some day. All the whites ain't low-down rats like Wilson.'

He left them and strode to his horse. He had mounted and was about to turn away when he looked back at the young Absarokee, who stood still with the Cheyenne arrow in his hands.

'How long since you seen that white man?'

The boy pointed to the sky, indicating where the sun would have been half-way through the forenoon.

'Since that of the sun.'

Elliot went on his way. So, Wilson was about three hours ahead and seemingly in not as much of a hurry as he had been if he felt he could waste time shooting at passing Indians. Maybe he believed that he had managed to leave Elliot well behind or, for some reason of his own, thought that Elliot would have chosen to follow the half-breed. Anyhow, it wouldn't be long before he was caught up with. Elliot spurred on the stallion, eager for that moment to arrive ....

Towards late afternoon, he came to a place where he could see the margin of the lake curving away out ahead of him. In the distance, he made out the shapes of two or three low buildings, derelict looking, like scraps of failed civilization left behind and forgotten in the wilderness.

In front of these, something white hung limply in the still air.

NINE

As he approached slowly through the long grass, between boulders and little clumps of trees, Elliot found that his view of the deserted farmstead – which was what it looked like from his first glimpse – was often obscured. At all times, he kept a sharp eye open for a possible attempt at ambush, and, at those places where there was too much cover just ahead, he took the time to make as wide a detour as he felt was necessary for maximum safety. Always, his eyes ranged ahead, measuring out the distance a rifle bullet could travel as opposed to a slug from a Colt .45.

At last, he held the buildings in clear view and he stopped to study them. As he had thought, they were derelict farm buildings – a cabin with its roof caving in, a broken-down barn, a shattered hen-coop. Some of the land round about had been cleared as a vegetable plot and was now knee-high in weeds. Some sod-buster had lived here and had probably worked himself to exhaustion before giving way to the forces of grinding poverty, sickness, maybe attacks, all these years ago, from marauding Indians ... or maybe the War had put a final end to the hopes of himself and his family.

Some distance in front of the cabin stood the crumbling remains of a wooden fence. A piece of planking had been leaned up against the end post, where a gate had been, and from it there hung the white object that Elliot had seen across the bend in the lake. It was a piece of white cloth, torn from a shirt or from underclothing, and evidently placed there to attract his attention.

To Elliot it looked like a badge of surrender.

He stared at it unbelievingly and then moved closer, his rifle already withdrawn from the saddle-boot and ready for action.

'Elliot!' The voice came high, desperate sounding, from the vicinity of the old cabin. 'Elliot – kin ya hear me?'

Elliot did not reply and remained still.

'Elliot! Don't shoot, Elliot! Kin ya hear?'

Elliot realized that he was probably just out of effective range from the Colt. The voice was muffled and seemed to come from within the walls of the cabin. Just behind the wall could be made out the shape of the hind-quarters of a bay horse, such as Wilson had ridden. The voice came again, louder, more insistent, like a man yelling with all the strength of his lungs.

'Kin ya not hear me, Elliot …?'

'I kin hear ya, skunk.'

'Listen, Elliot, I cain't go no further. I'm hit. Ya got me wi' thet bullet in the ravine. I'm bleedin' like a goddamn stuck pig. I give up!'

There was a silence, broken only by the faint lapping of the lake waters.

'If I come out, ya gotta promise thet ya won't shoot!'

A cricket called in the grass. Flies buzzed around the head of the black stallion.

'Elliot. I'm sorry 'bout the kid. It was just a kinda accident. It warn't no murder. He hung hisself. We was jest foolin' around. I'll stand trial – if thet's what ya want. Ya kin take me back to the sheriff.'

Wilson's horse moved to and fro, pawing the dirt restlessly.

'If I come out, Elliot, there won't be no shootin' …?'

'Sling out your gun and your belt.'

The gun-belt thudded out on to hard ground in front of the cabin. Elliot looked at it reflectively, Wilson's words going over in his mind. He remembered seeing Wilson jerk in the saddle as he rode out of the ravine, just when he, Elliot, had taken a quick shot at him. At the time, he had felt that Wilson had suffered only a slight nick at worst, but maybe he had taken a more severe wound – one that had become more and more serious with the long hard ride. Sometimes it happened that way. An untended wound could open up, wider and wider with the rough haste of a chase such as Wilson had just been through.

So now, he wanted to surrender. There was no more fight left in him and he was ready to take his chance with the law, although he was afraid of Elliot's vengeance. For the first time since setting out, Elliot felt uncertain as to what he should do about Jem's kidnapping and death. Always, he had seen himself shooting down all of these men, without hesitation and without pity. There was no pity in his heart now but there was a hesitation. It was to do with the white flag. Often in the War he had seen men surrender under a white flag – even if it was only an old piece of shirt – and it had been respected. They had been given their rights as prisoners of war. Only once had he seen a white flag not respected and he had looked down at the corpses and felt ashamed of the men whom he fought beside …. And it was to do with Campbell and his daughter. He knew what they would say if they had been here. 'Respect the law, Chris, because, without it, we've got nothing left … only the law of the gun, and that just puts everybody on the same perch as buzzards like Proctor and Wilson and Billy Wolf.'

He knew that they were right … but, in his own way, he had been right too. When the law was caught wrong-footed or was too slow to act, then you had to do what you thought was right, otherwise it was the evil men who came off best. But he could see that when they could be brought to a legal trial then it should be done, and it seemed that it was possible now to take in Wilson and let the law deal with him, as it should.

'Elliot! Kin I come out peaceable?'

'Yeah. Come on out with your hands high!'

'Ya won't do no shootin'? Give me your word, ya won't shoot!'

'Come out and don't make no trouble and ya won't git hurt!' Elliot's voice rose in irritation. To have this snake in the grass pleading for mercy was disgusting: to find himself agreeing to it was galling.

Wilson emerged, after some more hesitation, from the shelter of the cabin. He held his left hand up in a gesture of surrender, the other was in a sling suspended from his neck. He stumbled out, head and shoulders bent, like a man suffering with pain and fatigue.

'Turn around!' Elliot's order was curt and threatening.

Wilson remained still for a second, as if in sudden trepidation, and then turned slowly. Elliot rode up closer, slipped his rifle into the saddle-boot, drew Campbell's Colt and silently dismounted. He picked up the gun-belt and threw it to one side, well out of reach.

'OK. Turn around again.'

Elliot looked closely into Wilson's face. For a moment, the image of Jem came into his mind and he felt an impulse to smash this face with his gun but he restrained himself. Wilson stood, looking back at him with his eyes screwed up and his mouth twisted in an expression of pain. Elliot searched, though, behind the wrinkled eye-lids and did not see what he had expected. He had seen many men with gunshot wounds but had never seen one, with even a moderate wound, where the heavy calamity of it did not show in the eyes ... and it did not show in Wilson's eyes. They held no pain, no weight of prolonged suffering, no jitter of nerves, shattered and jumping ....

And the sling that held his arm was stained with the dry brownness of congealed blood, old and hard, and the shape did not look quite right, especially at the upper end, near the breastbone, where his injured hand was close to his chest.

And it was his right arm and hand which was in the

sling, his gun-belt carried the holster with its heavy Colt on the right side, and he had drawn from that side too in the street in Red Creek ... and just a few hours past he had been shooting at the defenceless young Indians.

So the oddly shaped lump in the sling was a hand which held a gun, not a heavy Colt, but one of a lighter calibre, equally deadly at close range ....

Elliot raised his gun two inches and his finger tightened on the trigger.

'Hold it there, Cavalry. I got ya covered, real good.'

The voice from behind was calm, almost soothing and somehow hypnotic, like a slithering snake, ready to strike. Elliot held his breath and made no movement. So it had all been a set-up ... the message on the stone, the white flag, a wide detour to come in behind him. And he had fallen for it, allowing himself to believe, against his better judgement, that such men could sometimes have a little regret for the crimes that they had committed.

Wilson's face split into a leering grin of yellow teeth.

'Didya really think, Elliot, that we was gonna ride outa here without that gold? Billy 'n me ain't so dumb ... but, by Gawd, you sure 'nuff are! Reckon you're 'bout as bird-brained as that lunkhead o' a brother o' yourn!'

Wilson gripped the gun and began to draw it out of the sling.

'Billy an' me's gonna find out all 'bout that gold. You got some talkin' to do, Elliot. Ain't that right, Billy?'

Billy Wolf did not reply. Wilson continued to pull gently on the gun under the sling. He thought he would draw it out slow and easy and watch the expression of surprise and dismay spread across Elliot's face as he realized how much he had been fooled. But the cloth of the sling had twisted itself just a little around the muzzle and it wasn't coming out too smoothly, although he knew, just a little tug would free it.

His eyes never left Elliot's face. He felt that he wanted to enjoy every fleeting moment of Elliot's discomfiture but Elliot did not look just the way Wilson had expected

and he still held the Colt pointed at Wilson's chest, and
he held it firm and steady. Also, there was an expression
on Elliot's face that Wilson had never seen on any man's
face before. It was an expression that carried a message
and the message came over loud and clear and
unmistakable.

And the message said: *You're the animal that murdered
my kid brother and this is the only chance I'm ever goin' to git to
kill you and I ain't gonna pass it up even though I know for
certain that it's the last thing I'll ever do!*

So, in a panic, Wilson tugged the gun free from the
sling but before he could raise it, he felt the thunder of
the impact of the Colt .45 bullet as it smashed through
his chest wall and it seemed as if a mule had suddenly
kicked his legs from under him and he hurtled
backwards and slammed his shoulders and head and
neck on to the hard, stony ground ....

Then it seemed as if a huge boulder had fallen from
the sky and lay across his chest so that he could not
move, but, after what seemed an age, he managed to
turn on his side and to raise himself up on to one elbow
and then up on to one knee and then on to the other,
and he knelt on the ground with his head hanging and
his arms drooping and the dirty rag with Billy's
congealed blood falling into the dirt and all his strength
seemed to be draining out of him, down his arms and
into the earth.

And then he looked up and saw, to his amazement,
that Elliot still stood with the gun in his hand as if, even
yet, Billy hadn't got around to shooting him.

Then he heard Billy's voice, clear and calm, but
somehow distant, as if it travelled through a long, long
ravine or a tunnel before it could reach him.

'I kinda figured ya might jest do thet, Cavalry ....'

Then he looked past Elliot to where Billy was standing
and he saw Billy's dark face suddenly split into that
quick grin of his and the voice came again, booming
through the tunnel. 'But it don't look ta me thet you've

made a real good job'v it!'. The muzzle of Billy's Colt appeared around the side of Elliot's elbow and Billy's voice seemed to rise in anger, a sudden blaze of anger, like something, long suppressed, which abruptly shook itself free, or like a burst of flame from the ashes of a forest fire which everybody thought had been stamped out, and when he gazed in astonishment at Billy, it seemed to him that the light eyes had turned dark, like those of an Indian, and that Billy Wolf looked more like an Indian than he had ever looked before, and the blazing voice from the tunnel shouted at him in a mad rage.

'You had it comin' to ya, Wilson! Ya shouldn't ever have done thet to the kid! The kid was somethin' special, Wilson, did ya know thet? He was a Crazy Man an' ya shouldn't ever have done him no harm! Ya don't kill a Crazy Man! But ya never understood thet, did ya, Wilson? Ya never ever understood nothin' in your whole goddamn life, ya dumb bastard ...!'

Then the entire universe turned into a sheet of searing red flame as the heavy Colt bullet from Billy's gun tore out his teeth and his lower jaw and all the lower part of his face, and the mass of red became a whirlpool which surged all around and around ... and the outer edges of the whirlpool turned to black and poured in upon him, like a flash flood in the mountains, and filled up all his inside with blackness, and choked and stamped the breath out of him, and the great boulder that Elliot had put on his chest rolled in with it and crushed him down and down into the dark so that he did not know about or feel Billy's next two bullets as they thundered and tore their way through his lungs and heart.

The silence hung in the air like a shroud. Elliot stared, somehow without feeling, at the hideous corpse before him. There was no sense of triumph or height of elation such as he had conjured up for himself when he had visualized the arrival of this moment when Jem's chief tormentor would lie dead at his feet. There was just an emptiness – and it was not because Billy Wolf had finished off what he had started, or because Billy Wolf still stood at his back with three bullets to spare – it was just the emptiness of the soul, and the sad vacancy of spirit which comes to most men when the act of revenge has been performed and is finished, still leaving its cause unmended.

'OK, Cavalry, slip thet gun back in its holster. He don't need no more bullets.' Billy Wolf sounded calm, self-satisfied, as if some little task, that needed doing, had been got out of the way.

'Now, jest raise your arms aways 'n walk over to thet wall. No hurry – slow 'n easy … OK, thet's far enough. Now turn around.'

When Elliot turned, he found that the half-breed had returned his own Colt to its holster and now stood, arms akimbo.

'When you're ready, Cavalry, draw …'

Elliot's hand flew for his gun but his fingers had scarcely touched the butt when he was looking straight down the barrel of his captor's Colt .45.

'Hold it! Right, jest drop the gun-belt 'n kick it thisaway. Thet's OK.' The Colt slipped back into the holster. 'Jest wanted ya t'know thet I ain't never met nobody quicker on the draw than me.

'Now then, you 'n me's had a tirin' enough ride last coupla days, Cavalry, and I reckon it's 'bout time we relaxed some. You git a fire goin' and I'll git coffee 'n whatever kinda chow ya got in this here saddle-bag out 'n ready for eatin'. Ya got more grub here than I seen in a week … and what 'bout this horse!' His voice rose in admiration. 'Didn't see this at your place. What happened to the grey?'

'Got itself shot,' answered Elliot, with some bitterness, 'along with a coupla your sidekicks.'

'Ya don't say.' Billy turned and looked at him, mouth and eyes creasing in amusement. 'Thet musta been

Lavelle 'n Pulley. Proctor was wonderin' where the hell they'd got to. Tell ya somethin', Cavalry, ya ain't jest so good with a side-gun, but ya kin sure use that ol' rifle. Thet shot ya finished off Proctor with was a real pleasure to behold!'

They sat over the fire in the evening air and sipped hot coffee and ate beans and pemmican and biscuit. Billy sat cross-legged, Indian fashion, and seemed, somehow, content and at ease with the world. He poked idly at the burning sticks and sometimes seemed lost in thought and, at other times, mumbled to himself, or engaged Elliot in conversation.

'Know somethin', Cavalry, I don't bear ya no grudges even though this here graze ya give me been burnin' like hell last coupla days. Reckon I'da done the same if I had been you. Only, if I'da got near enough to ya with a Colt, it woulda been no graze!' He laughed at his own joke. 'Fact is, I'm real sorry 'bout the kid. Didn't really mean thet to happen ....'

'You took him off!' snapped Elliot. 'What right do you have to bear grudges anyhow? If I'd blown your head into smithereens, ya would only have got what ya deserved ...!'

The half-breed looked at him in surprise for a second and then laughed.

'What you tryin' to do, Cavalry? Git yourself shot?' He shook his head and took another sip of coffee. 'Well, see, when I first met up with the kid, I reckoned he was jest a screwball, so I didn't have no conpunction 'bout takin' him to Proctor to answer a coupla questions 'cause I didn't think it mattered what the hell happened t'him anyways ... him jest bein' a goofy kid an' all ... but when we was all ridin' up thet there ol' gold trail, I see'd the kid sometimes goin' off inta a kinda dream, y'know, like a kinda trance, an' I remembered havin' heard tell in Red Creek how all the local Injuns used ta come in on their way by an' speak to him an' how they reckoned he was a kinda Crazy Man an' could speak to the spirits an' all ... and then, when Haze was hazin' him ...' – he grinned in amusement at his own unwitting pun – 'the kid says, jest like he was speakin' outa a dream, "When the conquerer is angry, his gifts are few". He says it, jest like thet. Like somebody or somethin' had put it inta his head. Now, thet's a real ol' Injun sayin', an' it sounded as if he was warnin' Haze thet there was some greater power thet would get even if Haze didn't leave off ... an' after thet, I got to rememberin' 'bout this ol' shaman in our village, who could read the signs, an' was allus sayin' things jest like thet, an' then I got to thinkin' 'bout my mother – she was Blackfoot, ya know thet, Cavalry? – I don't ever remember what happened to her. She was a good woman. We used ta sit in the tepee in the evenin' an' she would sing an' tell me all kinda stories 'bout the ol' days, when the Blackfeet was strong an' all the other tribes was afeared o' them ....'

He broke off and stared into the fire, as if his mind had drifted back to some age-old time, and he remained silent for many minutes, before taking up his monologue once again.

'The Blackfeet came from the far west, other side o' the Rockies. At the start, they was so far west thet the settin' sun, when it came down from the sky, used ta light their night fires ....' He glanced over at Elliot, as if expecting a denial, but Elliot remained impassive. 'Our first chiefs an' warriors came outa the rocks of the mountains. Ya kin still see their shapes, if ya look close. The mountain trees whisper all the time 'bout the deeds of our great nation an' spread their stories all over the world. Our huntin' grounds stretched for as far as the eagles could fly. We was great hunters, great warriors.'

He fell silent once more, staring morosely into the embers, and then began a scarcely audible chant in a half-remembered language, before his voice trailed off and he sat with closed eyes. He remained in this silent reverie for a long time, and it crossed Elliot's mind that he might take advantage of it, but a slight movement on his part brought the pale eyes staring, like an owl, and he knew that the half-breed, for all his mental distraction, still kept a close watch.

The fire had fallen low when Billy Wolf came back fully to reality.

'Cavalry, time we was turnin' in. Stand up. Put your hands toward me, full out. Thet's right.' A noose of cord was slipped around his wrists. 'Now move into thet cabin afore it gets too dark ta see, an' I'll tie up your legs for ya.'

The night went by in the greatest discomfort. Elliot lay, chafing in the tightness of his bonds, stiff and sore, with his mind troubled by what the morning might bring. Eventually, he fell into a restless sleep and was awakened by the sound of crackling wood as the half-breed relit the fire. After a time, he smelled coffee and Billy looked into the cabin with a cheerful grin.

'Breakfast jest about ready, Cavalry. I'll let ya walk up an' down a little ways – but don't try nothin'.'

The dream Indian of the evening before had gone, replaced by the outlaw, determined and ruthless.

After breakfast, Billy Wolf sat back and wiped his mouth with the back of his hand. He looked at Elliot contemplatively for a moment and then spat into the fire.

'Well, we ain't sittin' around here all day. Wilson was stinkin' even afore we shot him. Thing is, Cavalry, Wilson was jest about right with what he was sayin' yesterday – afore his jaw fell off with talkin'. We reckoned we had ta take ya in alive jest in case there was a chance thet ya know somethin' 'bout the gold ... nope, don't answer too quick – I ain't finished explainin' yet. I was thinkin' 'bout tellin' ya this last night so as ta give ya time ta think it over but I figured, what the hell, ya don't need more'n a coupla minutes ta make up your mind. Ya see, I been trailin' around with Proctor and his bunch of galoots for far too long and ain't never got nothin' out o' it but saddle-sores, hassle an' this goddamn rifle graze, an' I don't mind tellin' ya thet it sure gives me the bellyache ta end up with nothin' ta show for it.

'Now, Wilson reckoned from the start thet ya must know somethin' 'bout the gold 'cause your brother woulda told ya things thet he wouldn'ta said ta Proctor an' it seems ta me too, thet thet Cheyenne feller ya been keepin' company with mighta told ya somethin' as well.' He paused thoughtfully. 'What happened ta him, anyhow?'

'He decided to go back to his people.'

'Thet so? Well, I guess, he's lucky ta have people ta go back to. Tell ya somethin', though, Cavalry, if ya ever meet him again, tell him ta git himself a Colt .45 'stead o' thet beat-up ol' chunk o' ironmongery. Where in hell he git thet, anyways, find it in ...?'

'Git on with what ya was sayin',' interrupted Elliot, exasperated.

The half-breed looked surprised then shrugged his shoulders.

'You're sure in one helluva hurry ta hear the good news, Cavalry. OK, it's like this. I don't know for sure if ya know anythin' 'bout where thet gold's hid or not ... an' if I just ask ya straight out, I don't know if you're lyin'. So I figured thet the best way would be for ya ta know for certain thet ya got nothin' ta gain by keepin' quiet about it, 'cause ya won't live ta enjoy it. So I'm goin' ta ask ya a question an' the answer is either yeah or nope. If ya answer nope, then ya take a quick, easy bullet through the head an' won't hardly feel a thing. If ya answer yeah, an' you're lyin', then come sundown tomorrow, you'll be dead anyways, but you'll be so messed up thet compared ta you, Wilson, there, will look like the Sleepin' Beauty. If ya answer yeah, an' you're tellin' the truth, then you got my word, on my mother's grave – wherever thet is – thet you'll be walkin' back down thet valley ta Red Creek with no harm done ta ya. Only you'll have sore feet 'cause I can't let ya have a hoss if I'm gonna be sure o' a clean getaway. You understandin' all this, Cavalry?'

'I'm gettin' the idea ....'

'OK. So, the question is – are ya goin' ta lead me ta thet gold by tomorrow, sundown?'

'What if we cain't reach it by sundown?'

'I think it's at Dead Mouth. Thet's enough time ta git there. If it ain't there, well, I kin tell ya, I ain't gonna be led by the nose all around the goddamn country. It's gettin' too dangerous. Ya only got till sundown.'

'What if I don't know where the stuff is ...?'

'Well, answer nope an' take the bullet.'

'You think thet's some kind of a fair deal? You'll be killin' me for nothin' ...!'

'Who said anythin' about a fair deal? There ain't never been a fair deal in the whole world as far as I know. An' I told ya, the only way this is gonna work for me is if you know, for certain, thet ya cain't get out of it by lyin' an' tellin' me thet ya don't know where the gold is, so thet I'll let ya go, an' you'll come back later an' collect it. If thet gold ain't in my hands by tomorrow at sundown, then you're a dead man! If ya really don't know, then make it easy on yourself an' save my time by sayin' nope.'

Elliot stared at the half-breed. The man spoke as if he were presenting a perfectly reasonable solution to a slightly difficult problem and that any intelligent person would be sure to see its good sense. He was also in deadly earnest.

'Well, what's the answer, Cavalry? Yeah or nope?'

'Yeah, OK, I'll lead ya to the gold,' lied Elliot.

Billy Wolf looked at him for a moment, his features impassive.

'I reckoned ya would say thet, Cavalry. We'll soon see if you're tellin' the truth. One thing I allus noticed is thet most men'll cling on ta life for every last minute. I see'd men standin' under the gallows, scared as rabbits, but they seemed ta want ta spin even thet out, long as they could.'

He got to his feet and spat into the embers of the fire.

'Well, let's go. Sooner I git ta hell outa this country,

the better. I'm takin' the stallion. You kin ride my pony.
I turned Wilson's hoss loose this mornin' 'cause it's gone
lame and ain't worth two cents.'

So they began the long trail back the way they had
come. Elliot was forced to ride ahead, wrists bound so
that he was just able to handle the pony's reins, a rope
tied around his body with its end attached to the
pommel of the stallion's saddle, so that any attempt to
escape could result only in him being dragged to the
ground and shot where he lay.

To his surprise, he found Jem's wooden rifle hanging
from the pony's saddle and lightly nudging his knee as
he rode. The discovery sent a wave of emotion surging
through him as he remembered what this crazy gun had
meant to his brother; how Jem had cherished it, while,
he, himself, had been irritated by it .... But what was it
doing here, tied to the half-breed's pony? Well, he had
little difficulty in guessing the answer to that. He had
learned enough about Billy Wolf to know that he had a
belated respect for Jem as a Crazy Man, and that his
mind was as full of the superstitions of any redskin of
full blood whenever the mask of the white man slipped.
Billy Wolf, he knew, was a lost man, a man who felt
himself rejected by the world and who, in turn, rejected
it. The wooden rifle was some kind of a symbol to him, a
thing of the spirits, a sign of the Indian world to which
he felt he should belong but could not. And so, he had
picked it up from the scene of Jem's death. With
remorse? With anger? With some superstitious feeling
that it would bring luck to him? Who could tell?

'Where are ya leadin', Cavalry?' The voice, drawling
and relaxed jerked Elliot back to his present situation.

'Dead Mouth.'

'Ya got it right!' The half-breed laughed sardonically.
'Make sure we get there an' find what we's after.
"Sun-stones in Dead Mouth", like the kid said ... but the
stuff must be hid pretty good 'cause we searched from
one end to the other an' didn't find a damn thing!'

Elliot's eyes puckered. So Jem had said something about the gold to these men! Something about 'sun-stones' – gold nuggets – to be found in that ravine ... but how could he have known? Only through what had been said to him by the Cheyenne, obviously, and he had repeated it with no more sense and no more understanding than a mockingbird and had been condemned out of his own guileless mouth. But they had not learned enough to bring them to it and now Billy Wolf was playing his last card, in no way convinced that it would bring him his reward, but determined to play out the game until there was no more hope of winning.

And he, Elliot, would be that last losing card, crumpled and torn and thrown aside as the half-breed vented his anger and frustration and there was nothing he could do to prevent it. He knew nothing of the gold and every step on the trail brought him closer to that savage death.

A hundred times, as they rode through the long day, he racked his brain for some plan of escape, some means of turning the tables on his captor, but nothing came to his fatigued mind. The sleeplessness of the nights that had gone by stretched a web over his consciousness, dulling his senses and crippling his reason. The half-breed kept a grim silence too, as if anticipating the failure that awaited at the end of their journey, and nursing his determination to exact the cruel penalty he had promised.

Apart from two short halts to water and rest the horses, Billy Wolf allowed no respite until almost sundown. They made camp a few miles from the spot where Elliot had parted company from the Cheyenne and he fell into an exhausted sleep in spite of the tightness of his bonds. In the morning, he awoke, stiff and sore, and with the thought that this was his last day.

Billy Wolf made coffee and untied his captive so that he could drink and then walk up and down a little to ease his limbs. As he walked in a tight circle around the little camp, under the watchful eye of the half-breed, Elliot found his mind returning to its normal state of alertness, and with it a determination not to admit defeat but to be ready for any opportunity that might arise. In the end, he knew, he would turn and attempt to attack the half-breed, wrists still tied – as they probably would be – and his situation hopeless, but he would not stand like a steer, waiting to be poleaxed.

But that time was still some hours away and meanwhile he must do everything in his power to put Billy Wolf into a more relaxed frame of mind, in the hope – a very slim hope, certainly – that he might lower his guard.

Hypocrisy did not come easily to him, even in this desperate situation, but he felt that if he could appear more confident, as if he did not see death approaching at the end of the day, then it might seem to the outlaw that he must know where the gold was, after all. It might happen, then, that the grim tension, which had accompanied them on every step of the trail the day before, could become less acute and some slight carelessness might enter into Billy Wolf's attitude.

Elliot stretched his arms once again and forced himself to conceal his anger and hatred as he looked into the rugged and sinister features.

'I'll be goddamn glad when this is all over with, an' I kin git back to farmin'!'

'Yeah? Let's hope so ....'

'What say ya, we go fifty-fifty with the gold? Then we both git somethin' out of it.'

'No chance. Ya got your deal.'

'Looks like we got *your* deal. I ain't had any say ... but, OK, I got no room for argument. You mean it about lettin' me go, soon as I hand over the gold?'

'I nearly always mean jest what I say – unless I got a real good reason for sayin' the opposite – but I got nothin' against you, Cavalry, an' soon as I git the gold,

ou kin get ta hell outa my life an' back ta your
od-bustin'.'

As he spoke, the half-breed signalled for Elliot to
tretch out his arms in front so that they could be
ebound. The thought came that now might be the time
o attempt to grapple with the man but the look in Billy
Volf's eye told him that the slightest suspicious
novement or change of expression would be the signal
or that lightning-fast draw and the deadly rain of
ullets.

Elliot moved slowly over to the pony, his mind sizing
p the chances of leaping on its back in a crazy attempt
o gallop away before his captor could recover from his
urprise, but he dismissed the idea at once as madness.
Ie would be shot down within seconds and the fact that
e had even considered the action underlined to him
ne increasing sense of desperation which he was trying
o keep within bounds.

When he got to the pony, he noticed, once again, the
ooden rifle, hanging from the saddle. He stopped and
fted it in his cramped hands, his thoughts swinging
nomentarily from his own present danger to the
gonized death that Jem had suffered. How the
nnocent, foolish boy had valued this toy! Playing
round with it almost every day, carrying it everywhere!
nd what a childish mess he had made of it, with his
ndless notching, scratching and cutting. Often, Elliot
ad looked at it and shaken his head in amusement at its
untless marks, gathered over the years. The name
em', one of the few words its owner had learned to
rite, was scratched in clumsy lettering dozens of times
n its surface. Here and there were the crude shapes of
nimals or trees or people and, almost lost in this maze,
ere were little marks and signs carved out by Indians,
s they made a tentative request of the spirits for better
ealth or good luck in the future, believing – as many of
nem seemed to – that such a message, carried through
ne Crazy Man, would stand a better chance of being

listened to ....

And there, near the butt of the rifle, were some fresher marks, cut more neatly than Jem could ever have managed, which Elliot had never seen before.

Like most whites who have lived fairly close to Indians for much of their lives, Elliot knew a little Indian sign, not very much, but just enough to recognize a few of the symbols in front of him. There was the sign for the sun, connected by a stroke to another symbol which he did not know, the sign for mouth and for death, a mark which meant the number three and two others which meant nothing to him, the last one ending in a short scratch, as if the knife had slipped before it could be completed.

'All right, Cavalry, reckon you've stared at thet crazy gun long enough. We got to be movin'. Gimme it here.'

The wooden rifle was snatched from his hands and immediately thrust into the strap of the stallion's saddle-bag. Something about the half-breed's manner suggested something akin to embarrassment, as if he felt almost ashamed for being caught in possession of such a childish object.

They went on their way through the heat of the morning. Elliot's mind wrestled with the meaning of the signs he had read. 'Dead Mouth' was clear enough, the symbol for the sun and the other mark resolved themselves almost certainly, into 'sun-stones', the sign for 'three' could be applied to anything at all and the other marks, even after hours of thinking and guesswork, made no sense to him.

There was no doubt, however, who had put them there. Half Yellow Face had had the opportunity and the motivation. To cut the message in the magic rifle, to speak of it to the Crazy Man, was to put the secret of the gold into the hands of the spirits for their safe keeping.

Since then, the half-breed had searched for the gold for days, with the information as to its whereabouts at his hand. The irony of it brought a thin smile to Elliot's lips, although he realized that it would have been better for him if Billy Wolf had been more skilled at reading the Indian sign or had taken the time to disentangle the Cheyenne's message from the mess of cuts and markings which surrounded it. The gang would have found the gold and things would have turned out differently. He would not be riding along this trail to his death – but perhaps he would have been dead already and Wilson might still be alive. That would have been no better.

He was well aware, also, that he had learned little more from the Indian signs than he had known before. The gold nuggets were hidden in the ravine called Dead Mouth. Billy Wolf believed that already and he, Elliot, reckoned that it was probably true. Only the sign for 'three' gave him anything to go on ... but it could mean anything. Three trees? Three paces? Three years? There was no telling. Maybe if he had been given a longer look at the rifle he might have been able to work some sense out of it but he knew by the half-breed's attitude that the wooden rifle was going to stay in the saddle-bag, and to admit that he needed to examine the Indian signs because he did not know where the gold was hidden was to ask for death ....

In the late afternoon they passed the rotting and torn corpses of Proctor and the other two outlaws who had died near the entrance to the ravine. Billy Wolf grinned as he tied his bandanna over his nose and mouth.

'Hope to Christ, Cavalry, thet you're leadin' me straight ta thet there gold or pretty soon they'll be smellin' this place in Red Creek!'

TEN

The rock gullet of Dead Mouth opened to receive them, cutting off the light of the evening sun, casting deep shadows across their way. The silence of the death they had passed and that to come hung there in the dark folds of ancient stone, so that even the breathing of the horses and the sound of their hooves in the earth, seemed to disturb some age-old prehistoric grief which woke only at the approach of new tragedy and fresh despair.

The place was aptly named, not only because – like death – it seemed to lead, as far as mortal man could tell for sure, nowhere, but because its shadows seemed to lie in wait to envelop and to swallow all who ventured to pass its lips.

The gloom descended upon Elliot and bore down his spirit so that he was aware of the dire need to steady his nerves and to get a grip upon the fear that threatened to overwhelm him.

Now he was nearing the end of his journey of pretence. Within minutes, he must point out to the half-breed the exact spot where this seemingly mythical gold was hidden and when he did so, and was proved false, he would die, as certainly as the descending sun would make way for the night.

He was determined, still, not to surrender to the despair which rose around him like a thickening mist. Billy Wolf had forced this game of death poker upon him and therefore it must be played out until the last card was turned. The pretence must go on a little longer until two more cards had been played for what little they were worth ... one bearing the number three and the other, the joker – the final lie to persuade his opponent to lower his guard.

The number three, he had read in the Indian signs. It was the only new thing that the rifle had told him but he searched for it now with a diligence which he was obliged to conceal behind a mask of prior knowledge. His eyes scanned the towering sides of the ravine as they rode the narrow and broken track that twisted through its bottom. There seemed nothing to link with the vague, possibly misleading, clue that the signs had offered. There were clumps of gnarled trees and crippled, wasted bushes. Drifting scree slopes curtained the foot of rising, rugged cliffs. Large boulders, some of black basalt, strangely threatening in the dimming light, forced them into little detours as they made their slow progress.

They passed the entrance to the old mine, and Elliot cast a glance into its dark interior, wondering for a fleeting second whether to make this the place of his gamble. But there was no sign of three of anything there, just the remains of a crumbling barrow amid a long pile of debris.

With growing uncertainty, he nudged the pony onwards until he came to realize that they had travelled almost half the length of the ravine. At this point, the towering rock face dropped a little and the setting sun took a final glance across its edge, sending long shafts of fiery red to contrast with the black arrows of shadow created by the dark masses of standing stone.

Elliot blinked his eyes against the light. He knew that he could not go on much further. The half-breed had asked him no questions at all as to the exact whereabouts of the treasure, as if impatient with answers which might turn out to be lies, and preferring to wait until the gold lay before him before accepting that the truth had been told, or until his smoking gun pointed out his captive's dishonesty.

Nevertheless, more delay could only rouse suspicion, and suspicion must be allayed if there was to be any chance of a surprise move. He must pretend to have found the place, to have his hands untied so that he could work at uncovering the gold, to have the half-breed dismount, and then to leap forward with a stone or with his bare hands in a last hopeless struggle. Maybe he would be shot dead at once. That would be preferable to the fate he had been promised and to die making a last gesture of defiance was better than to cringe at the raised gun.

There was a dark shape just ahead of him. There was red light and deep shadow and the blackness of stone. His straining eyes took in the boulder of black basalt that lay in his path. It stood above the ground about waist high to a man. He had seen such isolated black boulders before, further back along the ravine floor ... and he thought he had seen two before and this was the third.

For a second, his heart leapt. Three! The number three! Three black stones. Could this be what had been written in the Indian signs which he had not been able to read? Well, he had read 'Dead Mouth' and he had read 'three' and this fitted, so maybe this had been meant. But he was not fool enough to believe it. There were a hundred other things that might have been referred to by the sign of three. Other objects which he had not seen; ideas and concepts which could not be seen ... but he could delay no longer. This must be the place of the final turn of the card.

'This is it.' He attempted to sound confident, sure of himself, almost casual, but he was aware of a less than convincing ring to his voice. 'Here – at this stone.'

For a moment Billy Wolf did not reply but when he eventually spoke, there was a detectable rise of excitement in his tone.

'You jest certain about this, Cavalry?'

'Yeah, this is the place all right. We gotta dig right here.'

'Dig?' the half-breed sounded faintly puzzled. 'How much diggin'?'

'Some.'

'OK. Git down off thet pony.'

Elliot dismounted, then he held up his bound hands.

'Cain't do a thing like this.'

The half-breed's knife flashed redly. The cords fell away. Elliot rubbed the feeling back into his wrists and then slackened off and removed the noose from his body. Billy Wolf made no objection but stared down at him expectantly. Elliot squinted back up at him, half-shielding his eyes from the sun.

'You'll need ta give me some help.' Elliot was aware of entering the final phase of the gamble. 'I cain't do it all by myself.'

'Seems ta me you'll have to.'

Billy Wolf moved the stallion a few more yards distance. He slid easily from the saddle and then stood, arms hanging loosely at his sides, his whole being relaxed and at ease but he did not come too close, and Elliot knew he was as watchful as ever.

'I got nothin' ta dig with.'

'Use your hands.' Billy grinned quickly, dark face splitting. 'Jest like an ole coyote. Don't seem ta me thet you'll need ta dig too deep. Thet stone ain't there fer nothin'.'

Elliot hesitated. Something in Billy Wolf's tone hinted at something he had not guessed at before. He put his hands out on to the rock. It seemed firm and solid as if it were an outcrop from the basalt seam below.

'Push it harder, for Christ sake, we ain't got all night. Put your weight on it an' it moves!'

Elliot pushed harder and felt the boulder give a little way. He stopped and looked straight at the half-breed.

'You knew thet? How come?'

'I tried it last time I was here. It's loose enough an' I'm

pretty sure ya kin shift it without no help from me. Like
I said, our deal still holds but one false move an' I'll kill
ya.'

'You tried this stone last time you was here?'

'Sure. Not so much thet Proctor an' his bunch could
see but 'nuff ta tell me thet what I read in the Injun sign
seemed ta be makin' sense. "Sun-stones buried under
third black stone in Dead Mouth" ... then somethin' else
thet your brother didn't git finished.'

'Ya knew all the time? You read the Injun sign?'

'Sure thing. Your brother musta wrote it on the rifle
an' I kin read most Injun sign better'n I kin read the
Bible.'

'Then what in hell did ya need me for?'

'The kid mighta wrote it wrong or it might be a lie, so
I reckoned thet I'd git you to lead me to it as well, then,
if you led me someplace different, I could look there
first an' if you was lyin', then I still got this place to try.
But ya led me straight to it, Cavalry, so I reckon it must
be here sure enough ....'

'Why didn't ya look here before?'

'I don't owe Proctor nothin'. When I saw I had got a
bit ahead o' him an' his bunch o' gophers, I reckoned on
keepin' the gold to myself. So I made sure thet I did the
searchin' around the black stones so thet nobody else
would be looking anywheres near it, then, when we all
cleared out, I'd give them the slip an' come back later.
But ya saved me a lot o' time by cuttin' right back on the
list of claimants, an' now thet we got rid of thet polecat,
Wilson, thet jest leaves you an' me ... an' you ain't got no
claim 'cause I got a gun and you ain't!' He laughed at his
own humour. 'But our deal still holds good. Ya played it
straight with me an' as soon as I have the gold, you kin
git on your way an' I'll git on mine, so jest put your back
into it 'cause I'm gittin' a little impatient.'

Elliot pushed harder at the stone. It moved
fractionally further and then began to rock gently to
and fro as he exerted more pressure upon it. It showed

no sign, however, of toppling over and after a time, he put his hands towards one end of it, applied all his weight, and found that it was beginning to slide around. It seemed to pivot as if it were standing on a very firm surface but only moved a few inches. He then pushed at the other end and gained a few inches more. Gradually, the stone slid from its original position. Elliot realised that with a little help, say with two men working on it, the boulder could have been shifted with relative ease, but Billy Wolf was standing well back, still obviously determined not to be taken off guard.

As the black stone moved aside, Elliot saw that it was not lying on the bare earth, but was resting upon another rock surface beneath. Soon this became exposed as a sandstone slab, about five or six feet in length and about a yard broad. As he scraped away some of the earth and pebbles around its edge, he discovered that it was only about three or four inches thick. He got to his knees and put his fingers under the edge of the slab and heaved it upwards. Soon it was balanced on its further edge and he was able to topple it over and it fell with a dull thud on the ground.

He noticed at once that the earth where it had lain had been recently disturbed. There was an area just at his hands where the ground was of a different colour and less firm than the immediate surroundings which had been compacted by years of bearing the weight of the stones. It was obvious that someone had been digging or turning the earth over very recently ....

His eye caught the corner of some half-buried object and his exploring fingers identified it as a short length of timber, a piece of planking, old and rotting. It had a damp feel about it and he felt the moss and lichen which clung to its edges which proved to him, at once, that it had lain or stood in the open for many years and not buried under the dark weight of the slab and the boulder.

As he drew out the wood, its passage disturbed

another object – a round edge, perhaps that of some container; in which the nuggets had been placed. His hand moved quickly to it, and then, as quickly, dropped the object as it appeared in the light, for it was a skull, its yellowing bone gleaming dull orange in eerie rays of the descending sun.

The unexpected shock sent a sensation of horror through his fingers and a cold shiver into his body. The perfect teeth of the skull grinned up at him, the empty eye sockets appeared to look at him questioningly. The cheek bones were prominent and broad and Indian-like. A length of black hair still clung to the cranium, stuck there by clay and pressure over the long years. It was braided in the style favoured by Indian women and decorated with tiny blue and white beads.

And there was a bullet hole in the temple.

For a long moment, Elliot knelt, staring at the grim object which he had unearthed. Then he became aware of a movement and a shadow behind him and he half turned his head to see Billy Wolf a few feet only away from him, as if compelling curiosity had drawn him into a proximity which he had been at pains to avoid.

The half-breed was quite still, his body bent over, almost in a crouching position, his legs spaced and tense, as if uncertain to move further forward or to leap back in sudden flight. His attention had been taken up entirely with the sight of the old, yellowing skull which lay before them and, as Elliot watched, the hard lines of the man's features began to melt and his mouth to sag, and his eyes opened in wide astonishment and fear, like a man who, for the first time, catches sight of some poltergeist which has haunted him throughout life.

Then his expression changed to one of terrible sorrow, and his eyes, usually so empty of feeling and always devoid of compassion, filled up with tears and his lips moved and shaped, over and over, a word which only slowly became audible, 'Mother, mother, my mother ....'

Amazed as he was by the half-breed's behaviour, Elliot, nevertheless, felt that this might be the chance he had been waiting for, and began to rise from his knees, ready to launch himself into attack, but Billy Wolf saw the movement and scampered back out of reach.

Then the half-breed's eyes fixed themselves once again on Elliot and the sorrow went from them and the tears burnt out in fierce anger. In a second, he held his knife in his hand, and he stood, legs spaced and balanced, head and shoulders stooped in the manner of an Indian brave preparing to duel to the death. The battered black hat had fallen from his head, the straggling hair hung across his face, and it was as if all the white had gone from him and the years had rolled back to the time of the Blackfeet and the old wars and the old wounds ....

'My mother. You killed my mother!' The hissing, hate-filled voice rose, trembling with near hysteria. 'Ya dragged her outa the tepee! Ya shot her! Ya lousy paleface dogs! She never did ya no harm – she never did nobody no harm but ya killed her! She was cryin' ... I was cryin' ... but it didn't make no difference. You was jest laughin'. Ya killed her fer nothin'. I remember her now! She was cryin' an' ya killed her ....' The old scar tissue, covering the mental wound, had burst and out came pouring all the sense of terrible loss and injustice, the bitterness and loathing that had festered there for so long. 'Ya low-down paleface coyote! You've had it comin' an' now I'm gonna tear your head from your shoulders ...!'

The knife arm came up. Elliot struggled to get to his feet. As he did so, the rotting wooden board he had just pulled from the soil which had been resting against his leg, fell to the ground with the side which had been flat to the earth now facing upwards. As he pushed himself up, Elliot caught a glimpse of the inscription which had been burnt in crude black lettering into its surface. It was a simple epitaph for this rough memorial which had

stood at this graveside during long years and was, for
some reason, now recently buried itself. It read:
'Sun-stones. R.I.P.'.

In that moment, he fought for his life.

The half-breed was upon him. Elliot sprang up barely
in time to grasp with both hands the arm that held the
murderous knife. The heavy rush of his opponent
almost knocked him from his feet but his slithering
boots found a steadying place and he held on grimly,
attempting to push the knife arm back ... back, back,
inch by inch, and to turn the blade in upon its owner.
For a brief moment, they pushed, one against the other,
and then Billy Wolf's left arm reached around Elliot's
neck and obtained a choking grip.

Elliot gasped, struggling and twisting against the pain
and the suffocation. The half-breed's face was almost
against his own and the savage teeth snapped wolf-like
while the mouth salivated and growled. The pale eyes
were wide and mad and bestial so that it was as if he was
engaged in a death struggle with some wild animal
instead of a human-being .... With all his strength, Elliot
forced the knife inwards and felt the point strike flesh.

The half-breed grunted and, for a second, slackened
his grip. Elliot twisted and pulled his neck free only to be
punched hard in the ribs. He pushed down desperately
on the half-breed's knife arm, attempting to knock him
off balance and to throw him but Billy Wolf kicked out
and they staggered to and fro until Elliot's heel struck a
stone and he fell heavily, jarring his arm against the
sharp edge of a rock and panting for breath as the
half-breed came down on top of him.

Elliot groped wildly for the arm that wielded the knife
but could find no grip. He sought to strike with his right
fist but the muscles in his arm seemed paralysed with the
blow he had just suffered. He heaved upwards, using
the strength of his legs and felt the half-breed slide to
one side and then roll a few feet clear.

Elliot began to struggle painfully to rise, fearful of

being leapt upon and knifed where he lay. All the breath had been knocked out of him but he thrust himself upwards and tried to prepare himself for the expected rush or to launch himself into the attack if his opponent was off guard.

He saw Billy Wolf get to his feet, shaking his head and spitting into the earth. The knife had fallen to the ground in the struggle and lay in plain view but, to Elliot's amazement, he ignored it, and, instead, picked up his battered black hat with its tattered feather and pulled it over his wild hair. As if prompted by an afterthought, he kicked the knife savagely to one side so that it lay well out of reach of them both.

He then straightened himself up, gasping still to regain his breath but seemingly unaware of the trickle of blood which ran down his thigh from the knife wound.

His eyes took in Elliot, the disturbed grave, the old skull, the short length of rotten wood. From where he stood, it was doubtful whether he could read the inscription on the latter but he had not shown any interest in doing so. Only the yellow skull with its bullet hole and trace of squaw hair had ripped into his mind to explode in insanity. But now the madness had gone from his eyes, which had turned cold and sharp and deadly cruel. They held an ice-cold anger of bitter resentment and Elliot knew that Billy Wolf felt betrayed – betrayed by the grave, by the old squaw-skull, by Jones, by the Cheyenne, by Proctor and his gang, by all the whites that ever lived and – most of all – betrayed by this sod-bustin', ex-cavalry bastard who had looked into his soul and seen his weakness ....

And Billy Wolf's pale eyes held the sentence of death, not the hot, savage death of angry conflict, but the cold, merciless death as meted out by the man who had lived all his life by the gun, the life-killer against whose sentence there could be no appeal as mercy was unknown.

And there came into the pale eyes that faint glimmer

which appears in the eyes of every gunman in that split
second between the thought and the act, and Elliot
caught that signal and saw himself as a dead man ....

Then the silent shadow of the lance stroked the red
light from Elliot's cheek and the lance flew as silently as
its own shadow. Only the grunting split of its impact was
heard as the fire-hardened point of the buffalo lance,
driven by its heavy shaft, punched its way between
yielding ribs and tore into the blood vessels of the heart.

For a second, Billy Wolf straightened up tall and then
arched backwards upon his heels, as if to distance
himself from the violence of the blow, before toppling
like a tree under the axe. He fell flat upon his back on
the stony ground, his arms widespread, fingers that had
clutched for the gun now spreading and stiffening, the
primitive lance shaft pointing his disturbed soul to the
sky. No sound came from his lips, only the pale eyes
stared, empty and pitiless.

For a moment, Elliot could not move. The shadow of
death had passed close by and his spirit still crouched
like a small bird under the flight of the hawk. This new
portrayal of death which lay in front of him, in this
grotesque shape and sudden barbarity, struck him into
still silence. For seconds, he could not believe that he was
still alive and that the fierce death which had stretched
out its hand towards him now lay lifeless, almost at his
feet.

Then a figure came bounding past him, only to
slacken pace and come to a halt beside the corpse. The
knife that had been raised to finish the grim task was
replaced in its sheath and a hand went out to grip the
wooden shaft and twist the lance from its bloody bed.

The shock of recognition pulled Elliot from his
momentary trance. Half Yellow Face stood over Billy
Wolf, eyes gleaming in triumph through the war-paint,
arms raising the lance in a gesture of victory.

At first, no words passed between them. The
Cheyenne looked towards Elliot but seemed not to see

him – as if his whole being had swelled to bursting point
in an ecstasy of triumph to the exclusion of all else. Only
by degrees did he descend to a calmer frame of mind
and then he smiled slightly and nodded as if greeting a
casual aquaintance.

Elliot was about to speak when he saw the Cheyenne's
expression change as he observed the disturbed grave.

'Horse Soldier,' the Indian's voice held a tremor of
superstitious dread. 'The spirit woman is awake.'

Elliot looked sharply at the fallen skull, gleaming
faintly in the shadows, then he understood and walked
over to the graveside. There, he dropped on to one knee
and pushed the macabre object back to its hiding place
in the soil. He smoothed over the earth and was about to
grip the sandstone slab when he realized that his right
arm was too stiff and sore to be effective. He motioned
for the Cheyenne to help him and, between them, they
replaced the slab and the basalt boulder. Then he lifted
the wooden board and, for some reason he did not quite
comprehend, set it upright as it might have been in the
past. With a slight ironic smile, he read the inscription
once again.

'Sun-stones, R.I.P.' Well, the wooden gun had not
lied, after all. Here was Sun-stones, buried in Dead
Mouth, just as had been scratched out in Indian sign,
not by Jem, as Billy Wolf had assumed, but by this
Indian who stood behind him now, who was fearless in
battle but scared of the spirits who kept him under
observation from the other world.

Elliot looked up at the Cheyenne, who seemed less
nervous now that the grave had been restored.

'Who was she, this Sun-stones? You knew her?' Elliot
watched Half Yellow Face flinch as he heard the dead
woman's name mentioned in such a bold and blatant
manner. After a moment's hesitation, the Cheyenne
attempted to explain in his halting English.

'This woman-squaw woman of Jones.' Elliot observed
that the Indian reluctance to speak the names of the

dead did not extend to the whites. 'She Cheyenne. Sister of my father. She live with Jones long time. Before big white war. Jones look for gold in this place. Big fight between gold men. She die. Jones bury her in this place. Jones come live with Cheyenne nation many year. Live with my father. They like brother. Long time ….'

Elliot nodded. He could just about see it all. The fight amongst the gold-hungry prospectors. Jones burying his wife here and then getting himself away from a situation that was becoming too dangerous. Going back to his Indian brother-in-law for some security, for a rest and a chance to think things out only to discover, as a good many whites had discovered before, that once the hospitality of the Plains Indians is accepted, it is by no means easy to walk away from it without causing grave offence – even to the point of a duel to the death.

So Jones had wandered for years with the Cheyenne, no doubt cursing – under his breath – ever having married the squaw woman, the one that he had called Sun-stones. Elliot smiled to himself. It was a good name for a prospector's woman. Maybe he had thought that she would bring him luck!

'Why did Jones come back here, Half Yellow Face? Why did you come with him?'

'My father die. Jones say squaw woman not sleep. He want see grave so she sleep easy ….'

The Indian turned away and paced slowly towards the dead outlaw. Elliot felt that he had left something unsaid, something in his mind which he did not know how to explain or did not wish to explain. The idea of the old prospector returning to his squaw-wife's grave for some superstitious or sentimental reason made little sense, but it might just have been a pretext to get himself away from his Indian relatives – an opportunity provided by the death of his redskin host and made easy by the gullibility of Half Yellow Face when presented with such arguments.

Anyhow, this was what it was all about – a red Indian

woman whose white husband had called her Sun-stones, out of his sense of humour or because he thought it might somehow change his fortunes, as the whites – in a less easily defined way – were often as superstitious as the Indians, whose beliefs they despised. This was what Proctor and his gang had struggled for and eventually died for; it was the reason why Billy Wolf lay with that gaping wound in his chest and why, in a twisted way, Jem had died too ....

The memory of Jem clouded his mind once again with sorrow. He shook his head and turned again towards the Cheyenne, who was standing over Billy Wolf, staring into the dead face.

'You saved my life,' Elliot somehow found it difficult to get his voice under control. 'Thank you.'

The remark seemed banal, crazy almost in the circumstances. He hesitated for a further moment and then walked over to the stallion where he drew out the cavalry rifle and all the ammunition he possessed and then returned. He held out the rifle almost ceremoniously, unconsciously imitating the Indian manner of presenting a gift.

'I want you to have this,' he said simply.

The Cheyenne looked at the rifle, then at him, then at the rifle again. For a second it seemed as if he would break out into a delighted smile but he did not permit the mask of gravity of the Indian warrior to slip. Only his shining eyes and a twitching at the corners of his mouth signalled his immense pleasure. He took the rifle with a faint inclination of the head and then hung it at the saddle of the half-breed's pony, which he evidently regarded now as part of the spoils of war. He then turned back to the corpse and bent over it with his scalping knife, while Elliot looked away, disgusted at the mutilation but understanding well enough the redskin reasoning behind the act.

Shortly afterwards, they moved off down the ravine, Elliot mounted on the stallion, while Half Yellow Face rode his own pony and led that of Billy Wolf behind. The shadows had deepened and the Indian seemed now to be in a hurry to quit the place, looking about often as if he expected the restless spirit of his aunt to emerge from the darkness at any moment.

As they came out of the mouth of the gorge, passing the huddled shapes that were the remains of the Proctor gang, Elliot remembered Billy's remark as they had entered Dead Mouth, just before sundown, and for the first time, felt a sense of profound relief flooding through him, as if realizing fully how close he had been to death. The thought brought with it a feeling of elation and he grinned quietly to himself, curbing a sudden urge to yell out as the tension of the last two days released him from its death grip.

He was struggling with these emotions as Half Yellow Face pushed his pony into the lead along the widening track, still discernible in the fading light. As he rode behind the jogging ponies, Elliot found questions rising in his mind which demanded answers, but something about the tense preoccupation of the silent Indian, the gloom that was settling all around and the stillness of the night air prevented him from speaking.

After travelling in this silence for a long distance, Half Yellow Face drew to a slow halt at a place where a silver birch gleamed weirdly in the faint twilight. Here, he twisted in the saddle to look back at Elliot as if to make some comment, but appeared to change his mind, and slipped to the ground instead. Elliot saw him stoop and pull aside some stones or other debris, then came the sound of some heavy object being dragged out of the earth and the Indian turned around to face him, his arms around a dark bundle. The Cheyenne's voice was low, half whispering.

'In this place, Jones take sick. Put gold in ground.'

'Gold?' Elliot's eyes widened in the darkness, straining to see. 'There was gold, after all …?'

He dropped to the trail and approached as the

Cheyenne lowered the weight of the bag on to a stone. Elliot stared closely at the faint gleam. His fingers explored the hard surfaces of the rugged irregular nuggets ....

'The sun-stones. Ya had them all the time!'

'No.' The Indian shook his head emphatically. 'Spirit woman lie with gold. Long years ... Jones say spirit not sleep with gold. Bad medicine. We come here. Jones take gold from grave. Squaw spirit sleep peaceful.'

Elliot stood dumbfounded, his mind wrestling to unravel the rest of the story. So, Jones had buried his gold along with his squaw all those years ago. To hide it from the greedy eyes of his fellow miners? Or because it was not rightfully his? No doubt, he had intended coming back for it at a much earlier date than he had managed but extended Indian hospitality had seen to it that he had languished out on the plains with his Cheyenne friends and relatives instead of enjoying the profits of his hard work or his treachery. Anyway, he had got back too late to do himself any good, in spite of the trust and loyalty of his Indian companion, who did not know quite enough about white people to realize that when it comes to gold they will lie even to their friends.

'What happened to Jones, Half Yellow Face?'

'He take sick. Then bad men kill. Now bad men dead. War-path ended. You take gold.'

The offer was made in the same flat monotone as the rest of his short, clumsy explanation. It was as if the Cheyenne wanted this tedious matter out of the way with all speed.

'It ain't mine to take, Half Yellow Face. If it belongs to anybody it belongs to you.'

'Gold no good for Indian. Bad medicine for Indian.'

Well, he knew that much, at any rate. The possession of gold could bring nothing but trouble to an Indian. White avarice would see to that. At best, he would be robbed; more likely, he would be murdered or accused of theft and hanged. The gold was bad medicine for the Cheyenne – maybe it was bad medicine for everybody. So far, it had been for Jones, his squaw, for Proctor and his gang and most of all for Jem. But it made no sense to leave it where it was. Superstition was no substitute for reason. The gold could be used for good as well as for evil.

His mind was still troubled as he lifted the bag and carried it to the stallion. Its weight and feel told him that he held a fortune in his hands. He placed it in his emptied saddle-bag and drew the straps tight. When he turned around, he saw that the Indian had remounted and was ready to depart. Elliot hurried to him, holding out his hand in friendship. The Cheyenne shook hands and Elliot could sense the pleasure that the redskin felt at the gesture and his satisfaction in Elliot's acceptance of the gold. Elliot realized that the Cheyenne regarded it as a gift given in return for the prized rifle and he remembered that, amongst the Plains Indians, a present of great value must be met by another of equal value to avoid a loss of prestige on the part of the receiver. He had not thought that he had taken a risk of offending Half Yellow Face with his gift of the rifle, but the risk had been there.

He knew too that the lance had not struck down Billy Wolf in order to save his own life. That had been more or less incidental to the act of revenge for the death of Jones, who – whatever else he was – had been a blood brother of the revered father.

'Horse Soldier, I go to my people. Here is this. Light Eyes carried this. It is of your brother, the Crazy Man.'

Elliot looked through the half light at the wooden rifle which had hung from the half-breed's saddle. Something in the Cheyenne's tone told him of the esteem in which the object was held. To the Indian, it was a sacred symbol to be cherished. Elliot smiled up at him.

'Keep it. Remember that, to the white man, the gold is worth many rifles, whether they kin shoot or whether they kin only do other things – like this magic rifle.' His voice trailed off a little as he remembered how magic the rifle had been to Jem all his life. 'I'd like you to have it. Maybe it'll be good medicine.'

'Thank you, Horse Soldier.'

The little wooden gun was slipped into the rope loop that had lately carried the ancient rifle of the spirit father, which had brought near disaster to its owner. For some reason that he was not quite clear about, Elliot put his hand on it for a moment.

'Listen, Half Yellow Face, why did ya come back? Ya said the war-path was all bad medicine. All the spirit signs told ya.'

The Cheyenne bent down from the saddle. Elliot could just make out his eyes gleaming in a kind of wild triumph.

'Signs change. Absarokee come to kill Half Yellow Face. Absarokee die. Cheyenne medicine again strong. Spirit Father speak. Say go back to war-trail.' He straightened up and held the buffalo lance against the night sky. Elliot could see that two scalps had now been attached to it. One was wild and ragged, like the hair of Billy Wolf, the other seemed smoother, braided and youthful. This one, the Cheyenne stroked almost lovingly for a few seconds. 'Absarokee boy very brave. Come like wildcat to kill. Shoot arrow, throw lance but Half Yellow Face too strong, too good a warrior. Cheyenne medicine very strong.'

He lowered the lance and then pulled something from his belt. He passed it down to Elliot who felt its shape and saw the white of the striped wild turkey feathers glowing faintly.

'This arrow belong you. Maybe you lose on trail.' There was a faint hint of doubt in his voice, some trace of unspoken suspicion. 'Absarokee boy shoot but Cheyenne arrow not kill Cheyenne. Maybe boy find arrow, maybe steal?' He laughed softly in the darkness. 'Maybe Absarokee think arrow strong medicine to kill

Cheyenne. Give courage. Make fight like wildcat ....
Goodbye, Horse Soldier.'

He nudged his pony into motion and moved off down
the trail. Elliot watched the dim shapes of the Cheyenne
and the ponies vanish slowly into the dark and heard,
for a long time, the hoofbeats grow fainter in the
distance. When he eventually aroused himself to action,
he found that he had broken the arrow in his tense
hands. He threw the pieces into the darkness and
turned to the restless stallion.

He rode the tiring animal at a slow walking pace
through the night. The moon arose and lit the trail ahead
but he scarcely noticed its coming. All his mind was a
turmoil of mixed emotion and troubled thought. It
seemed to him that too often it was the young and the
innocent and the brave who paid the penalty for human
greed and pride and foolishness. Jem, because he was
dragged into a quagmire of avarice and brutality created
by vicious men; the young Absarokee, because of tribal
pride and tradition and ancient feuding and because he
had been pointed to his death by the unwitting act of the
white man whom he had come to believe was his friend.
At least, that was how it appeared to be. A score of times,
Elliot asked himself whether the boy would have
attacked an older, stronger and more experienced
warrior if he had not been given the encouragement of
believing that his medicine was strong – that the arrow
and the white man's words would somehow bring him
victory. It was impossible to be sure and he would never
know for certain. In a way, the uncertainty made it more
difficult to accept.

Anyhow, the young man was now dead, and if he had
not died, then Half Yellow Face would not have
returned to the war-trail and he, Elliot, would now be
lying in Dead Mouth, a stiffening corpse or still dying
from the cruel bullets of his enemy. Billy Wolf would be
on his way to commit more crimes and the Cheyenne
would be on his way home, with fewer scalps to boast of

but with less blood on his hands.

Did any of it make any sense? Elliot was aware of the same feelings of helplessness and hopelessness that had dogged him on his cavalry patrols and in the aftermath of battles. In his mind's eye, the faces of long-dead comrades sprang up before him. He remembered them as mostly young and cheerful and easy-going but they had killed and died for dim ideals and the world did not seem any the better for their sacrifice.

He thought, too, of Billy Wolf, that half-crazy man, the offspring of two different cultures, two different ways of thinking, who had come to believe that he belonged to neither and who was haunted also by a hideous memory, buried in fear by his childhood mind, yet lurking there in the dark to burst out in savagery when the grave of the squaw woman had been opened … and all that had had its effect upon Billy Wolf, making his life what it was, as one evil act gives birth to a hundred more.

He knew that he should stop and rest but he could not do so. There was too much darkness all around and death still hung in the night air.

The sun was beginning to rise when he slid from the saddle, took a careful moment to ground tether his mount, and then fell into a deep sleep in the grass beside the trail. When he awoke, he felt much refreshed and his dark thoughts, like the night, had receded. Not that any of it could be forgotten, and he knew that there must be further sorrow and grief and perhaps remorse, but like a man who finds a foothold on the slippery bed of a stream, he knew that he could withstand the cold current of past events which could not be altered and would not be overwhelmed by them.

He stood up and stretched his muscles, breathing in the morning air with a sense of quiet pleasure. The stallion stood half asleep and he remembered with a feeling of rising satisfaction that he would have to ride down the valley and return it to Campbell.

When he was there, he knew that he would see the girl and that she would be glad to see him. Her eyes had told him that when he had last looked into them and he had to admit to himself that he would be glad to see her also. For some reason that he could not figure out it seemed easier to admit to such feelings than it had been before. Somebody had kicked down a door in his mind and air was blowing through, somehow fresh and liberating.

There was a breeze blowing from the west also. It stirred needs that had long been suppressed and he knew that there was a new life out there and that he could ride out to meet it and that it promised all he had ever wanted … and he felt pretty sure that the girl would come with him.

In fact, he was certain that she would! He rubbed his jaw thoughtfully as he began to work out in his mind what he would say to her first chance when they were on their own – but, snakes alive! – maybe he should get himself a shave first!

He grinned and walked over to stroke the nose of the black stallion. As he did so, he looked out over the tumbling hills to the west. He could see a long, long way and for the first time in years he knew where he was going.